FIVE ARE TOGETHER AGAIN

FIVE ARE TOGETHER AGAIN

ENID BLYTON

Illustrated by
Eileen A. Soper

Hodder
Children's
Books

a division of Hodder Headline plc

Text copyright © Enid Blyton Ltd.
Illustrations copyright © Hodder & Stoughton Ltd.

Enid Blyton's signature and the Famous Five are
registered trademarks of Enid Blyton Ltd.

First published in Great Britain in 1962
by Hodder and Stoughton

This hardback edition 1998

For further information on Enid Blyton, please contact
www.blyton.com

10 9 8 7 6 5 4 3 2 1

A Catalogue record for this book is available from the
British Library.

ISBN 0-340-70431-4

Typeset by Hewer Text Composition Services, Edinburgh
Printed and bound in Great Britain by
Clays Ltd, St Ives plc

Hodder Children's Books
a division of Hodder Headline plc
338 Euston Road
London NW1 3BH

CONTENTS

1	BACK FOR THE HOLIDAYS	1
2	PLANS FOR THE FIVE	11
3	BIG HOLLOW – AND TINKER AND MISCHIEF AGAIN!	20
4	JENNY HAS A VERY GOOD IDEA	29
5	THE TRAVELLING CIRCUS	40
6	GETTING READY FOR CAMPING OUT	50
7	IN THE CIRCUS FIELD	60
8	CHARLIE THE CHIMP IS A HELP!	69
9	A WONDERFUL EVENING	78
10	ROUND THE CAMP FIRE	88
11	IN THE DARK OF THE NIGHT	100
12	A SHOCK FOR TINKER	110
13	QUITE A LOT OF PLANS!	121
14	LADDERS – AND A LOT OF FUN!	133
15	A HAPPY DAY – AND A SHOCK FOR JULIAN	143
16	NIGHT ON KIRRIN ISLAND	154
17	AND AT LAST THE MYSTERY IS SOLVED!	167

CHAPTER ONE

Back for the holidays

'GEORGE, CAN'T you sit still for even a minute!' said Julian. 'It's bad enough to have the train rocking about all over the place, without you falling over my feet all the time, going to look out of first one window and then the other.'

'Well, we're nearly at Kirrin – almost home!' said George. 'I can't *help* feeling excited. I've missed old Timmy so *much* this term, and I just can't *wait* to see him! I love to look out of the window and see how much nearer we are to Kirrin. Do you think Timmy will be on the station to meet us, barking madly?'

'Don't be an idiot,' said Dick. 'He's a clever dog, but not clever enough to read railway timetables.'

'He doesn't need to,' said George. 'He *always* knows when I'm coming home.'

'I really believe he does,' said Anne, seriously. 'Your mother always says how excited he is on the day you are arriving home from school – can't keep still – keeps going to the front gate and looking down the road.'

'Dear, dear Timmy!' said George, falling over Julian's feet again, as she scrambled once more to the window. 'We're nearly there. Look, there's the signal-box, and the signal is down. HURRAH!'

1

FIVE ARE TOGETHER AGAIN

Her three cousins looked at her in amusement. George was always like this on the way home from school. Her thoughts were full of very little else but her beloved Timmy all the way home. Julian thought how much she looked like a restless boy just then, with her short, curly hair, and her determined expression. George had always longed to be a boy, but as she wasn't, she made up for it by trying to speak and act like one, and would never answer to her full name of Georgina.

'We're coming into Kirrin station!' yelled George, almost falling out of the window. 'I can see Peter, the guard. Hey, we're back again. WE'RE BACK AGAIN!'

The train slid into Kirrin station, and Peter waved and grinned. He had known George since she was a baby. George opened the door and leapt out of the carriage.

'Home again! Back at Kirrin! Oh, I do hope Timmy will be at the station!' she said.

But there was no Timmy there. 'He must have forgotten you were coming,' said Dick, with a grin, and at once got a scowl from George. Peter came up, smiling all over his face, and gave them his usual welcome. Everyone in Kirrin village knew the Five – which, of course, included Timmy the dog.

Peter helped the children with their luggage, and wheeled it down the platform on his trolley. 'Had a good term?' he asked.

'Fantastic!' said Dick. 'But it seemed very long, as Easter is so late this year. Gosh – look at the primroses on the railway banks.'

BACK FOR THE HOLIDAYS

But George had no eyes for anything just then. She was still looking out for Timmy. Where was he? WHY hadn't he come to the station to meet them? He came last time and the time before! She turned a troubled face to Dick.

'Do you think he's ill? she asked. 'Or has he forgotten me? Or . . .?'

'Oh, don't be silly, George,' said Dick. 'He is probably in the house somewhere and can't get out. Look out – the trolley nearly ran you over then.'

George skipped out of the way, glaring. WHERE was Timmy? She was sure he was ill – or had had an accident – or was tied up and couldn't get away. Perhaps Joanna, who helped her mother in the house, had forgotten to let him loose.

'I'm going to take a taxi home, if I've enough money,' she said, taking out her purse. 'You others can walk. I must see if anything's happened to Timmy – he's *never* missed meeting our train before.'

'But George, it's such a lovely walk to Kirrin Cottage!' said Anne. 'You know how you love to see your island – dear old Kirrin Island – as we walk to your mother's house – and the bay – and hear the waves crashing on the rocks.'

'I'm taking the station taxi,' said George, obstinately, counting the money in her purse. 'If you'd like to come with me, you can. It's Timmy I want to see, not islands and waves and things! I'm SURE he's ill or has had an accident or something!'

'All right, George, do as you please,' said Julian. 'Hope

3

you find dear old Timmy is perfectly well – and has only forgotten the time of the train. See you later.'

The two brothers and their sister Anne set off together, looking forward to the walk to Kirrin Cottage. How lovely to see Kirrin Bay again, and George's island!

'Isn't she lucky to have a real island of her very own!' said Anne. 'Fancy it belonging to her family for years and years – and then one day her mother suddenly gives it to George! I bet she worried and worried dear Aunt Fanny until she gave in to old George. I do so hope Timmy is all right; we shan't enjoy our holidays with George's mother if there's anything wrong with Timmy.'

'Oh, George will probably go and live in Timmy's kennel with him,' said Dick, with a chuckle. 'Ha – look! The sea – and Kirrin Bay – AND the little old island as lovely as ever!'

'With its gulls circling round, and mewing like cats,' said Julian. 'And the old ruined castle there, just exactly the same as usual. Not a single stone fallen out of it, as far as I can see.'

'You can't *possibly* see that at this distance,' said Anne, screwing up her eyes. 'Oh, isn't the first day of the hols heavenly? We seem to have all the time in the world in front of us!'

'Yes. But, after a few days, the holidays *rush* by,' said Julian. 'I wonder if George is home by now.'

'Well, her taxi passed us going at a tremendous pace!'

said Dick. 'I bet old George was shouting at the driver to go as fast as possible!'

'Look – there's Kirrin Cottage – I can just see the chimneys in the distance,' said Dick. 'Smoke is coming from one of them.'

'Funny – why only one?' said Julian. 'They usually have the kitchen fire going, and a fire in Uncle Quentin's study. He's such a cold mortal when he's working out all his wonderful figures for his inventions.'

'Perhaps he's away,' said Anne, hopefully. She was rather afraid of George's hasty-tempered father. 'I should think Uncle Quentin could do with a holiday at times – he's always buried in rows and rows of figures.'

'Well, let's hope we don't disturb him too much,' said Julian. 'It's hard on Aunt Fanny if he keeps yelling at everyone. We'll try and be out of doors most of the time.'

They were nearly at Kirrin Cottage now. As they came near to the front gate, they saw George come running down the garden path. To Julian's horror, she was crying bitterly.

'I say – it does look as if something has happened to old Timmy,' he said. 'It's not like George to cry – she *never* cries! What *can* have happened?'

In great alarm they began to run, and Anne shouted as she ran, 'George! George, what's the matter? Is something wrong with Timmy? What's happened?'

'We can't stay at home,' wept George. 'We've got to go away somewhere. Something awful's happened!'

BACK FOR THE HOLIDAYS

'What is it? Tell us, you idiot!' said Dick, in alarm. 'For goodness' sake, what's happened? Is Timmy run over, or something?'

'No – it isn't Timmy,' said George, wiping her eyes with her hand, because, as usual, she had no handkerchief. 'It's Joanna – Joanna, our dear, darling Joanna!'

'What's the matter with her?' asked Julian, thinking of all kinds of dreadful things. 'GEORGE, will you please TELL US!'

'Joanna's got scarlet fever,' said George, sniffing dolefully. 'So we can't be at Kirrin Cottage.'

'Why not?' demanded Dick. 'Joanna will have to go to hospital – and we can all stay at Kirrin Cottage and help your mother. Poor old Joanna! But cheer up, George, scarlet fever isn't much of a thing to have nowadays. Come on – let's go in and see if we can comfort your mother. Poor old Aunt Fanny, she *will* be in a stew – with all of us four cousins at Kirrin Cottage too! Never mind, we can . . .'

'Stop jabbering, Dick,' said George, exasperated. 'We *can't* stay at Kirrin Cottage. Mother wouldn't even let me go in at the front door! She shooed me away, and said I was to wait in the garden, the doctor was coming in a minute or two.'

Someone called to them from a window of Kirrin Cottage. 'Are you all there, children? Julian, come here, will you?'

They all went into the garden, and saw their Aunt Fanny, George's mother, leaning out of a bedroom window.

'Listen, dears,' she said. 'Joanna has scarlet fever, and is waiting for an ambulance to take her to the hospital, and . . .'

'Aunt Fanny – don't worry. We'll all turn to and help,' called back Julian, cheerfully.

'Dear Julian – you still don't understand,' said his aunt. 'You see, neither your uncle nor I have had scarlet fever – so we are in quarantine, and mustn't have anyone near us, in case we get it, and give it to them – and that might mean we'd give it to all you four.'

'Would Timmy get it?' asked George, still sniffing dolefully.

'No, of course not. Don't be silly, George,' said her

8

mother. 'Did you ever hear of dogs getting measles or whooping-cough or any of *our* illnesses? Timmy isn't in quarantine. You can get him out of his kennel as soon as you like.'

George's face lit up immediately, and she shot round the back of the house, yelling Timmy's name. At once there came a volley of barks!

'Aunt Fanny – what do you want us to do?' asked Julian. 'We can't go to my home, because Mummy and Daddy are still in Germany. Should we go to a hotel?'

'No, dear, I'll think of somewhere you can all go,' said his aunt. 'Good gracious, what a row Timmy is making! Poor Joanna – she has such a splitting headache.'

'Here's the ambulance,' cried Anne, as a big hospital van drew up outside the gate. Aunt Fanny disappeared from the window at once to tell Joanna. The ambulance man went up to the front door, his mate behind him carrying a stretcher. The four children watched in surprise. 'He's gone to fetch dear old Joanna,' said Julian. And sure enough the stretcher was soon carried out with Joanna lying on it, wrapped round in blankets. She waved to the children as the men carried her out.

'Soon be back!' she said, in rather a croaky voice. 'Help Mrs Kirrin if you can. So sorry about this!'

'Poor Joanna,' said Anne, with tears in her eyes. 'Get better quickly, Joanna. We shall miss you so!'

The ambulance door closed and the van went off very smoothly and quietly.

'Whatever shall we do?' said Dick, turning to Julian. 'Can't go home – can't stay here! Oh, here's TIMMY! How are you, Tim, old thing? Thank goodness *you* can't get scarlet fever. Don't knock me over, old boy. Down! Gosh, what a licky dog you are!'

Timmy was the only one in high spirits. The others felt really down in the dumps. Oh dear – what was to be done? Where could they go? What a horrid beginning to a holiday! Down, Timmy, DOWN! What a dog! Anyone would think he had never even *heard* of scarlet fever! WILL you get down, Timmy!

CHAPTER TWO

Plans for the Five

GEORGE WAS still looking upset. What with her fears that Timmy might be ill or hurt, and now her distress at Joanna being carried off in the ambulance, she wasn't much help to anyone.

'Do stop sniffing, George,' said Anne. 'We've just got to be sensible and think of some way out of this.'

'I'm going to find Mother,' said George. 'I don't care if she's in quarantine or not.'

'Oh no you're not,' said Julian, taking her firmly by the arm. 'You jolly well know what quarantine means. When you had whooping-cough *you* weren't allowed to come near any of us, in case we caught it too. You were infectious, and that meant that you didn't have close contact with anybody for at least a few weeks. I think it's only two weeks for scarlet fever, so it won't be too bad.'

George went on sniffing, trying to pull away from Julian's hand. Julian winked at Dick, and said something that made George pull herself together at once.

'Well, REALLY, George!' he said. 'You're acting *just* like a weepy girl. Poor Georgina! Poor little old Georgina!'

George stopped sniffing immediately and glared at

Julian in fury. If there was one thing she really hated it was
to be told she was acting like a silly *girl*! And how *awful* to
be called by her real name, Georgina! She gave Julian a
hefty punch, and he grinned at her, warding her off.

'That's better,' he said. 'Cheer up! Just look at Timmy
staring at you in amazement. He's hardly ever heard you
crying before.'

'I'm NOT crying!' said George. 'I'm – well, I'm upset
about Joanna. And it's awful to have nowhere to go.'

'I can hear Aunt Fanny telephoning,' said Anne, who
had very sharp ears. She fondled Timmy's head, and he
licked her hand. He had already given everyone a wonderful welcome, whining with pleasure, and licking lavishly.
He had been mad with joy to see George again, and was
surprised and sad to find her looking so miserable now.
Dear Timmy – he certainly belonged to the Five!

'Let's sit down and wait for Aunt Fanny,' said Julian,
settling himself on the grass. 'We look a bit silly standing
staring at Kirrin Cottage like this. Aunt Fanny will come
to the window in a minute. She is sure to have thought of a
good idea for us. TIMMY! I shan't stay sitting down for
long if you keep licking my neck like that. I shall send you
for a towel in a minute, so that I can wipe it dry!'

The little joke made everyone feel better. They were all
sitting on the grass now, and Timmy went lovingly from
one to the other. All his family back again – it was too
good to be true! He settled down at last, his head on
George's knee, George's hand caressing his ears.

PLANS FOR THE FIVE

'Aunt Fanny's put down the telephone,' said Anne. 'Now she'll come to the window.'

'You've got ears like a dog – just as good as Timmy's,' said Dick. '*I* couldn't hear a thing!'

'Here's Mother!' said George, and leapt to her feet as Aunt Fanny came to the window and leaned out.

'It's all right, dears,' she called. 'I've been able to arrange something for you. I have been telephoning the scientist that your father has been working with, George – Professor Hayling. He was coming here for a day or two, and when I told him he couldn't, because we're in quarantine, he at once said that *you* must all go *there* – and that Tinker, his son – you remember him, don't you – would be delighted to have your company!'

'Tinker! Goodness, yes, I shall never forget him – or his monkey either!' said Julian. 'He's the boy who owns that old lighthouse at Demon's Rocks, isn't he? We went to stay there with him, and had a marvellous time.'

'Well – you're not staying at the lighthouse, I'm afraid,' said his aunt, from the window. 'Apparently a storm blew up one night and damaged it, and it's not safe to live in any more.'

Groans from all the Five, of course, Timmy joining in as usual! 'Where are we to go then? To Tinker's *home*?' said Dick.

'Yes. You can get a bus from here, at Little Hollow, that will take you almost to Big Hollow, where Professor

Hayling lives,' said Aunt Fanny. 'You're to go today. I'm
so very sorry about this, dears, but it's just one of those
things we have to put up with. I'm sure you'll have a good
time with Tinker, and that monkey of his. What was it
called now?'

'Mischief,' said everyone together, and Anne smiled in
delight to think of being with the naughty little creature,
and watching its wicked ways.

'The bus will pass in ten minutes,' said her aunt. 'And
have a good time, dears, and send me a card or two. I'll let
you know how we get on – but I really don't think that
either your uncle or I will catch scarlet fever, so don't
worry. And I'll send you some money to spend. You'd
better run for the bus now.'

'Right, Aunt Fanny, and thank you!' called Julian. 'I'll
look after everyone and keep them in order – especially old
George. Don't worry at all – and I do hope you or Uncle
don't go down with the fever. Goodbye.'

They all went to the front gate where the luggage still
stood. 'Anne, go out into the road and stop the bus when it
comes,' ordered Julian. 'Then Dick and I will heave our
bags aboard. Gosh, I wonder what it will be like with old
Tinker at Big Hollow. I've a feeling it might be rather
exciting!'

'*I* don't think so,' said George, mournfully. 'I like
Tinker all right – he's funny – and that little monkey is
a darling – such a *naughty* little thing too. But oh dear,
don't you remember what it was like when Tinker's *father*

14

came to stay with us? It was *awful*! He never remembered to come to meals, and was always losing his coat or his hanky or his money, and losing his temper too. I got very tired of him.'

'Well, he'll probably get very tired of *us*!' said Julian. 'He won't find it very funny to have four kids parked on him, especially if he's in the middle of difficult work – to say nothing of a rather large, licky dog leaping round the house as well.'

'Timmy isn't likely to lick *him*,' said George, at once, and put on one of her scowls. '*I* didn't like Tinker's father at all.'

'Well, don't look like a thunderstorm,' said Julian. 'I don't expect he'll like any of *us* either. But it's kind of him to let us come and stay at Big Hollow, and we're jolly well going to behave ourselves, see? There's to be no back-chat from *you*, George – even if he dares to disapprove of Timmy!'

'He'd better *not*,' said George. 'In fact, I've a good mind not to go. I think I'll live in the summer-house with Timmy, at the bottom of the garden!'

'You will NOT!' said Julian, taking firm hold of her arm. 'You'll play fair, come with us, and behave properly! Listen, there's the bus. Come on, we'll all wave, and hope there are a few empty seats.'

Anne had already stopped the bus, and run round to ask the driver if he would help with the bags. He knew the children very well, and leapt down at once.

FIVE ARE TOGETHER AGAIN

'You're going back to school pretty quick!' he said. 'I thought the schools had only just broken up.'

'They have,' said Julian, 'but we're off to stay at Big Hollow. The bus goes there, doesn't it?'

'Yes, we go right through the village of Big Hollow,' said the driver, carrying three bags at once, much to Julian's envy. 'Whereabouts are you staying there?'

'At Professor Hayling's house,' said Julian. 'I think that's called Big Hollow too, like the village.'

'Ah, we pass it,' said the driver, 'I'll stop the bus just outside and give you a hand with your things again. My word – you'll have to mind your ps and qs there – old Professor Hayling's a bit peculiar, you know. Goes off the handle properly if things don't go his way! Once a horse got into his garden and believe it or not he chased that horse for two miles, shouting at it all the way. And bless me, when he got back home, tired out, there was that horse, chewing up his garden again. The horse was cute – he'd taken a short cut back. Yes – you be careful how you behave at Big Hollow. The old man might get cross and pop you into one of his strange machines and grind you up into little pieces!'

The four children laughed. 'Oh, the old Professor is all right,' said Julian. 'A bit forgetful, like most people who work with their brains all the time. My brain goes fairly slowly – but my Uncle Quentin's goes about a hundred miles an hour, and I bet the Professor's does too! *We'll* be all right!'

PLANS FOR THE FIVE

Away went the bus, bumping over the road from Kirrin and Little Hollow, and on to Big Hollow. The four children gazed out of the windows as they passed alongside the shore, where the sea shone as blue as cornflowers, and once more saw Kirrin Island out in the big bay.

'Wish we were going *there*!' sighed George. 'We'll have to take a picnic meal there sometime, and enjoy ourselves. I'd like old Tinker to visit my island. He may have a lighthouse of his own, but having an island is MUCH *better*!'

'I think I agree with you,' said Julian. 'Tinker's lighthouse is certainly lovely and all on its own, and the view from it is amazing – but there's something about Kirrin Island that I *love*. Islands are quite different from anything else!'

'Yes. They are,' said Anne. '*I'd* like one too. A very little one, so that I could see all round it at one glance. And I'd like one little cave to sleep in – just big enough for *me*.'

'You'd soon be lonely, Anne,' said Dick, giving his sister a friendly pat. 'You love to have people round you, you like to be friendly!'

'So does Timmy!' said Julian, as Timmy left his place by George's knee and went to sniff at a string bag held by an old man, who at once fondled the big dog, and fumbled for a biscuit out of a paper bag. 'Timmy doesn't mind how many people there are around, so long as one or two of them have a biscuit or a bone to hand out!'

FIVE ARE TOGETHER AGAIN

'Come to heel, Timmy,' said George. 'You're not to go round begging, telling people you are half-starved! I should think you eat more than any other dog in Kirrin. Who eats the cat's dinner whenever he can, I should like to know?'

Timmy gave George a loving lick and settled down beside her, his head on her toes. He got up politely every time someone entered or left the bus. The driver was most impressed.

'I wish all dogs were as good on my bus as yours,' he told George. 'You'd better get ready to jump out. Our next stop is supposed to be a little way beyond Big Hollow, but I'll stop for a moment, and you can get out.'

PLANS FOR THE FIVE

'Thanks a lot,' said Julian, gratefully, and when the bus stopped with a jerk a minute later, all the Five were ready to jump out.

The bus went on, and left them standing outside a large wooden gate. The drive from it led steeply downwards, and a large house could just be seen hidden in a hollow by great trees.

'Big Hollow!' said Julian. 'Well – here we are. What a strange place – sort of mysterious and brooding. Now to find old Tinker! I bet he'll be pleased to see us all, especially Timmy! Help me with the bags, Dick!'

CHAPTER THREE

Big Hollow – and Tinker and Mischief again!

THE FOUR children and Timmy went through the big heavy gate, which groaned loudly. Timmy was very startled to hear the mournful creak, and barked sharply.

'Sh!' said George. 'You'll get into trouble with the Professor, Timmy, if you raise your voice like that. I expect we'll have to talk in whispers, so as not to disturb the Professor – so just see if you can whisper too.'

Timmy gave a small whine. He knew he couldn't whisper! He trotted at George's heel as they all went down the steep drive to the house. It was a curious house, built sideways to the drive and had astonishingly few windows.

'I expect Professor Hayling is afraid of people peering in at his work,' said Anne. 'It's very, very secret, isn't it?'

'I know he uses miles and miles of figures,' said Dick. 'Tinker told me one day that his monkey Mischief once chewed up a page of figures when he was very small – and Professor Hayling chased him for a whole hour, hoping to catch him and find even a *few* bits of paper still in his mouth, so that he could rescue at least part of his figures. But Mischief fled down a rabbit hole and didn't come up for two days, so it wasn't any good.'

20

Everyone smiled at the thought of poor Mischief hiding down a rabbit hole. '*You* couldn't do that, Timmy old thing!' said Julian. 'So just be careful of any paper *you* eat.'

'He wouldn't be so silly,' said George, at once. 'He knows perfectly well what's eatable and what's not.'

'Ha! *Does* he!' said Anne. 'Well, I'd just like to know what kind of food he thought my blue slipper was that he chewed up last hols!'

'Don't tell tales on him,' said George. 'He only chewed it because someone shut him in your bedroom and he hadn't anything else to do.'

'Woof,' said Timmy, quite agreeing. He gave Anne's hand a little lick, as if to say, 'Very sorry, Anne – but I was so *bored*!'

'*Dear* Timmy! I wouldn't mind if you chewed up *all* my slippers!' said Anne. 'But it would be nice if you chose the very *oldest* ones!'

Timmy suddenly stopped and looked into the bushes. He gave a low growl! George put her hand on his collar at once. She was always afraid of snakes in the spring-time.

'It might be an adder!' she said. 'The dog next door trod on one last year, so I heard, and his leg swelled up terribly, and he was in great pain. Come away now, Timmy – it's an adder, with poison in its fangs!'

But Timmy went on growling. Then he suddenly stood still and sniffed hard. He gave an excited whimper and pulled away from George, jumping into the bushes – and

21

out came, not a snake, but Mischief, Tinker's bright-eyed little monkey!

He at once leapt on to the dog's broad back, put his little monkey fingers under Timmy's collar, and chattered in delight. Timmy nearly dislocated his neck to twist his head round to lick him!

'Mischief!' cried everyone at once, in real delight. 'You've come to welcome us!'

And the little monkey, jabbering away excitedly in monkey language, leapt first on to George's shoulder, and then on to Julian's. He pulled Julian's hair, twisted his right ear round, and then leapt from him to Dick, and on to Anne's shoulder. He cuddled into her neck, his eyes bright and brown, looking very happy.

'Oh! *Isn't* he pleased to see us again!' said Anne, delighted. 'Mischief, where's Tinker?'

Mischief jumped off Anne's shoulder and scampered down the drive as if he quite understood all that Anne had said. The children raced after him – and then a loud voice suddenly roared at them from one side of the drive.

'What are you doing here? Clear out! This is private ground. I'll fetch the police. Clear OUT!'

The Five stopped still in fright – and then Julian saw who it was – Professor Hayling! He stepped forward at once. 'Good afternoon,' he said. 'I hope we didn't disturb you, but you did tell my aunt we could come here.'

'Your aunt? Who's your aunt? I don't know any aunt!' roared the Professor. 'You're sightseers, that's what you are! Come to pry into my work, just because there was a piece about it in some silly paper! You're the third lot today.

Clear out, I tell you – and take that dog too. How DARE you!'

'But – don't you *really* know us?' said Julian very startled. 'You came to stay at our house, you know, and . . .'

'Stuff and nonsense! I haven't been away for years!' shouted the Professor. Mischief, the monkey, was so frightened that he leapt away into the bushes, making a funny little crying noise.

'I hope he fetches Tinker,' said Julian, in a low voice to Dick. 'The Professor has forgotten who we are, and why we've come. Let's retreat a bit.'

But as they went cautiously back up the steep path, followed by the angry Professor, a loud voice hailed them, and Tinker came racing up with Mischief on his shoulder, clinging to his hair. So the little monkey had gone to fetch him. Good for *him*! thought Julian, pleased.

'Dad! Don't yell at our friends like that!' cried Tinker, dancing about in front of his angry father. 'You asked them here yourself, you know you did!'

'I DID NOT!' said the Professor. 'Who are they?'

'Well, George, that girl, is the daughter of Mr Kirrin, and the others are his niece and nephews. And that's their dog, Timmy. And you asked them all here because Mr and Mrs Kirrin are in quarantine for scarlet fever,' shouted Tinker, still dancing about in front of his father.

'Stop jigging about like that,' said the Professor, crossly. '*I* don't remember asking them. I would have told Jenny the housekeeper if I had.'

BIG HOLLOW

'You did tell her!' shouted Tinker, still jigging about, with Mischief the monkey jigging too in delight. 'She's angry because you left your breakfast and now it's almost dinner time. She's cleared it away.'

'Bless us – so *that*'s why I feel so hungry and cross!' said Professor Hayling, and he began to laugh. He had a tremendous laugh, and the children couldn't help laughing too. What an odd fellow – so brainy, such a fine scientist – with the most enormous amount of knowledge in his head – and yet no memory for such ordinary things as breakfast and visitors and telephone calls.

'It was just a misunderstanding,' said Julian, politely. 'It was very, very kind of you to invite us here when we can't be at home because of the scarlet fever. We'll try not to be a nuisance, and if there's anything we can do to help you, please ask us. We'll make as little noise as possible, and keep out of your way, of course.'

'You hear that, Tinker?' said Professor Hayling, suddenly swinging round on the startled Tinker. 'Why can't you do the same – make very little noise, and keep out of my way? You know I'm very busy now – on a MOST IMPORTANT project.' He turned to Julian. 'You'll be very welcome if you keep Tinker out of my way. And NOBODY – absolutely NOBODY – is to go up into that tower. Understand?'

They all looked up to where he was pointing, and saw a tall, slender tower rising up amid the trees. It had curious tentacle-like rods sticking out at the top, and these shook slightly in the breeze.

'And don't ask me questions about it,' went on the Professor, looking fiercely at George. 'Your father's the only other man who knows what it's for, and *he* knows how to keep his mouth shut.'

'None of us would *dream* of prying,' said Julian. 'It's very, very kind of you to offer to have us here, and do believe me when I say we shan't be any trouble to you at all – but a help if you'll allow us.'

'Ah well, you sound a sensible fellow, I must say,' said the Professor, who had now calmed down, and looked quite peaceable. Well, I'll say goodbye for now and go and have my breakfast. I hope it's fried eggs and bacon. I'm very hungry.'

'Dad – Jenny's cleared your breakfast AWAY! I told you that before!' said Tinker in despair. 'It's almost dinner-time, now.'

'Ah good – good!' said the Professor. 'I'll come at once.'

And he led the way indoors, followed by the five children, with Timmy and Mischief, all looking rather worried. Really, nobody *ever* knew what the Professor was going to do or say next!

Jenny certainly had a good dinner for them all. There was a large and delicious stew with carrots, onions and peas swimming in the gravy, and plenty of potatoes. Everyone tucked in well, and Mischief, who loved the peas, took quite a few from Tinker's plate, his little paw creeping up, and neatly snatching a pea from the gravy.

The girls went out to help bring in the next course, which was a big steamed pudding with plenty of raisins in it. Mischief at once jigged up and down in delight, for he loved raisins. He leapt on to the table, and received a sharp smack from the Professor, who unfortunately smacked the pudding dish at the same time, making the pudding jump in the air.

'Good gracious, Dad – we nearly lost the pudding!' cried Tinker. 'And it's my favourite. Oh, don't give us such *small* pieces! Mischief, get off the table. You are NOT to put your paw into the sauce!'

So Mischief disappeared under the table, where he received quite a lot of raisins from various kindly hands, unseen by the Professor. Timmy felt rather left out. He was under the table too, having been rather scared by the Professor's angry voice, but as he didn't very much like raisins, he wasn't as lucky as Mischief.

'Ha – I enjoyed that!' said the Professor, having cleaned his plate thoroughly. 'Nothing like a good breakfast!'

'It was midday dinner, Dad!' said Tinker. 'You don't have pudding at breakfast.'

'Dear me, of course not – that was pudding!' said his father, and laughed his great laugh. 'Now you can all do exactly what you like, so long as you do NOT go into my study, or my workroom, or that tower. AND DON'T MEDDLE WITH ANYTHING! Mischief, get off the water jug, you'll upset it. Can't you teach that monkey some table manners, Tinker?'

27

And with that he marched out of the room, and disappeared into some mysterious passage that apparently led to his study or workroom. Everyone heaved a sigh of relief.

'We'll clear away and then I'll show you your rooms,' said Tinker. 'I do hope you won't find it too dull here.'

Dull, Tinker! You needn't worry! There is far too much excitement waiting for the Five – and you too! Just wait a bit, and see!

CHAPTER FOUR

Jenny has a very good idea

TINKER RACED out to the kitchen to fetch a tray or two. He made a most peculiar noise as he went, and for a moment Timmy looked extremely startled.

'Goodness – don't say that Tinker *still* has that awful habit of pretending to be some kind of car!' groaned Julian. 'How on earth does his father put up with it? What's he think he is now? A motorbike by the sound of it.'

There was a sudden crash and a loud yell. The Five raced down the kitchen passage to find out what had happened, Timmy at the front.

'Accident!' bellowed Tinker, scrambling up from the floor. 'I took the bend too quickly, and my front wheel skidded, and I went bang into a wall! I've bent my mudguard.'

'Tinker – do you mean to say you're *still* being silly enough to pretend to be cars and motorbikes and tractors and lorries?' demanded Julian. 'You nearly drove us all mad, driving about all over the house, when you stayed with us. Have you *got* to be a machine of some sort?'

'Yes,' said Tinker, rubbing one of his arms. 'It sort of

29

comes over me, and away I go. You should have heard me yesterday, being a lorry absolutely *loaded* with new cars for delivery. Dad *really* thought it was a great lorry and he rushed out into the drive to send it away. But it was only me. I hooted too – like this!'

And the sound of a loud and a deep hooter immediately filled the passage! Julian shoved Tinker into the kitchen and shut the door.

'I should have thought that your father would have been driven completely mad by now!' he said. 'Now, you just shut up. Can't you grow up a bit?'

'No,' said Tinker, sullenly. 'I don't want to grow up. I might be like my father and forget to eat my meals, and go out with one sock on and one off. And I'd hate to forget my meals. Just think how *awful* it would be! I'd always be hungry.'

Julian couldn't help laughing. 'Pick up your tray, and help to clear away!' he said. 'And if you simply can't HELP being a car sometimes, for goodness' sake go outside! It sounds terrible in the house. You're much too good at awful noises.'

'Oh, am I *really* good?' said Tinker, pleased. 'I suppose you wouldn't like to hear me being one of those new planes that go over here sometimes, making a funny droning noise?'

'No, I WOULD NOT!' said Julian, firmly. 'Now will you PLEASE get that tray, Tinker. And tell Mischief to get off my right foot. He seems to think it's a chair.'

FIVE ARE TOGETHER AGAIN

But Mischief clung to Julian's ankle and refused to move. 'All right, all right,' said Julian. 'I shall just have to walk about all day with you riding on my foot.'

'If you *stamp* as you walk, he soon gets off,' remarked Tinker.

'Why didn't you tell me that just now?' asked Julian, and stamped a few steps round the room. Mischief leapt off his foot at once and sat on a table, making an angry noise.

'He sits on Dad's foot for ages, even when he walks about,' said Tinker. 'But Dad doesn't even notice him there! He even sat on Dad's head once, and Dad thought he was wearing his hat indoors and tried to take it off. But it was only Mischief there!'

That made everyone laugh. 'Now come on,' said Julian, briskly. 'We really must clear away the dinner things. We three boys will carry out the loaded trays and you girls can wash up. And DON'T let Mischief think he can carry teapots or milk jugs.'

Jenny was very pleased with their help. She was short and fat, and waddled rather than walked, but managed to get here and there remarkably quickly.

'I'll show your visitors their bedrooms after we've cleared,' she said. 'But, you know, Tinker, those mattresses we sent to be remade haven't come back yet. I've told your father a dozen times to telephone about them, but I'm sure he hasn't remembered.'

JENNY HAS A VERY GOOD IDEA

'Oh JENNY!' said Tinker, in dismay. 'That means that the two beds for visitors can't be slept in! What ever are we to do?'

'Well, your Dad will have to ring up for new mattresses to be sent today,' said Jenny. 'Maybe they would send them out by van.'

Tinker immediately became a furniture van and rushed down the passage, into the dining-room and back again, Mischief following him in delight. He made a noise exactly like a slow-moving van, and the children couldn't help laughing.

The Professor shot out of his study, his hands to his ears. 'TINKER! COME HERE!'

'No thanks,' said Tinker, warily. 'Sorry, Father. I was a van bringing the mattresses you forgot to order for the beds for visitors.'

But the Professor didn't seem to hear. He advanced on Tinker, who fled upstairs with Mischief leaping after him. Professor Hayling turned on Jenny.

'Can't you keep the children quiet? What do I pay you for?'

'Cleaning, cooking and washing,' she said, briskly. 'But I'm not a nurse for children. That Tinker of yours could do with half a dozen nurses, and he'd still be a nuisance to you while he was in the house. Why don't you let him take his tent and camp out in the field with his friends? It's hot weather and those new mattresses haven't come, and they'd all love it. I can cook for the

33

children and take them out meals – or they could come and fetch them.'

The Professor looked as if he could give Jenny a big hug. The children waited eagerly to see what he would say. Camping out – that would be fun in this weather – and honestly, living in the same house as the Professor wasn't going to be much fun. Timmy gave a little whine as if to say 'Fine idea! Let's go at once!'

'Good idea, Jenny, VERY good idea!' said Professor Hayling. 'But that monkey's to camp out too. Then perhaps he won't jump in at my workroom window and fiddle about with my models!'

He marched back into his study and slammed the door so hard that the whole house shook. Timmy was startled and gave a yelp. Mischief the monkey leapt up the stairs again, howling in fright. Tinker began to dance round in joy, and very firmly Jenny took hold of him and propelled him into her big, clean kitchen.

'Wait, Jenny, I've remembered something. We've only one tent, and that's mine, a small one. I'll have to ask Dad if I can get two big ones!' And before anyone could stop him he was banging at the Professor's door, then flung it open, and shouted out his request.

'WE WANT TWO MORE TENTS, DAD. CAN I BUY THEM?'

'For goodness sake, Tinker, clear out and leave me alone!' shouted his father. 'Buy SIX tents if you want them, but GET OUT!'

JENNY HAS A VERY GOOD IDEA

'Ooh, thanks, Dad!' said Tinker, and was just slipping out of the door when his father yelled again.

'But what on earth do you want TENTS for?'

Tinker slammed the door and grinned at the others. 'I'd better buy Dad a new memory. He's only *just* told us we can camp out, and he knows there's only my very small tent – almost a toy one.'

'I'm glad we shan't be in the house,' said Anne. 'I know what a nuisance it is to *George's* father to have us around, playing about. We'll be better out of the way.'

'Camping out again!' said George, very pleased. 'Let's catch the bus back home and get our own tents. I've got them all stored away in the garden shed. We can just ask Jim the carrier to take them in his van, when we've found them.'

'He's calling here today – I'll give him the message for you, if you like,' said Jenny. 'The sooner you get the tents, the better. It was a kind thought of the Professor's to ask you all here, but I just knew it wouldn't work! You'll be all right out in the field at the back of the house – he won't hear a thing, not even if you all yell together! So you get your tents and put them up, and I'll see what I can find in the way of ground-sheets and rugs.'

'Don't bother, Jenny,' said Julian. 'We've got all those things – we've often camped out before.'

'I only hope there aren't any cows in the field,' said

Anne. 'Last time we camped, a cow put its head into my tent opening, and mooed. I woke up with such a jump, and I was too scared to move.'

'I don't think there are any cows,' said Jenny, laughing. 'Now I MUST get on with the washing-up, so will you bring out the dinner things please – but don't let that monkey carry anything breakable, for goodness sake! He tried to balance the teapot on his head last week – and that was the end of the teapot!'

Soon everyone was hard at work, clearing away, and helping Jenny with the washing-up.

'I shall like camping out,' Anne told her. 'I'd be scared of staying here in the house. Professor Hayling is a bit like my Uncle Quentin, you know – forgetful, and quick-tempered and a bit shouty.'

'Oh, you don't want to be scared of him,' said Jenny, handing Anne a dish to dry. 'He's kind, for all his crossness when he's upset. Why, when my mother was ill, he paid for her to go into a really good nursing-home – and believe it or not, he gave me money to buy her fruit and flowers!'

'Oh goodness – that reminds me – we MUST send Joanna some flowers,' said George. 'She has scarlet fever, you know. That's why we're here.'

'Well, you go and telephone the florist,' said Jenny. 'I'll finish this job.'

But George was rather afraid that Professor Hayling might rush out to see who was using the telephone!

JENNY HAS A VERY GOOD IDEA

'I'm sure we can buy flowers in Kirrin village, and have them sent,' she said. 'We've got to go and get our things ready for Jim, and I can order the flowers then. We might as well come back on our bicycles – they'd be useful here.'

'Well, you'd better go now,' said Jenny, 'or you won't be back in time for tea, and *then* there'd be trouble.'

'*I'll* bring back Anne's bicycle,' said Julian. 'I can easily manage it beside mine as I ride back.'

'Look, George,' said Dick, 'you needn't come. I'll order the flowers and I can bring your bike back too. So you stay with Anne.' Reluctantly George agreed.

Off went Julian and Dick, leaving Tinker and the girls to help Jenny. But Jenny soon sent Tinker off, afraid that he would drop things and break them.

'You go and be a nice, quiet, purring Rolls-Royce at the bottom of the garden,' she said. 'And when you think you've done thirty miles or so, come back for petrol.'

'Lemonade, you mean!' said Tinker, with a grin. 'All right. I haven't been a Rolls-Royce for a long time. Dad won't hear me right at the bottom of the garden!'

Off he went, and Jenny and the girls finished the washing-up. Mischief was a nuisance and went off with the teaspoons. He leapt to the top of a high cupboard, and dropped them there.

Tinker suddenly put his head in at the window. 'Come on out to the field where we're going to put up our tents,' he called to Anne and George. 'We'll choose a nice sheltered spot. Buck up! You must have finished washing-up by now. I'm tired of being a Rolls-Royce!'

'You go with him, Anne,' said George. 'I don't feel like it just now.'

So down the garden went the two children and out through a gate at the bottom into a big field.

'Good gracious!' said Tinker, staring. 'Look at all those caravans coming in at the gate the other end of the field. I'll soon send them off. It's OUR field!' And away he marched to the gate in the distance.

JENNY HAS A VERY GOOD IDEA

'Come BACK, Tinker,' shouted Anne. 'You'll get into trouble if you interfere. COME BACK!'

But Tinker marched on, his head held high. Ha – he'd soon tell the caravan folk it was HIS field!

CHAPTER FIVE

The travelling circus

ANNE WATCHED anxiously as Tinker went on and on over the field. There were now four caravans trundling in the far gate, and behind them, in the lane, were vans – enormous vans – all with enormously large words painted on them.

TAPPER'S TRAVELLING CIRCUS

'Hoo! I'll tell Mr Tapper what I think of him, coming into *my* field!' said Tinker to himself. Mischief the monkey was on his shoulder, jogging up and down as Tinker marched along, muttering furiously.

Four or five children from the caravans looked at him curiously as he marched along. One small boy rushed up to him, shouting in delight to see the monkey.

'A monkey, look, a monkey!' he cried. 'Much smaller than our chimp. What's he called, boy?'

'Mind your own business,' said Tinker. 'Where's Mr Tapper?'

'Mr Tapper? Oh, you mean our grandad!' said the boy. 'He's over there, look, beside that big van. Better not talk to him now. He's busy!'

THE TRAVELLING CIRCUS

Tinker walked over to the van and addressed the man there. He was rather fierce-looking and had a long, bushy beard, enormous eyebrows that hung down over his eyes, a rather small nose, and only one ear. He looked inquiringly down at Tinker, and put out his hand to Mischief.

'My monkey might bite you,' said Tinker, at once. 'He doesn't like strangers.'

'I'm no stranger to *any* monkey,' said the man, in a deep-down voice. 'There's isn't a monkey in the world, nor a chimp either, that wouldn't come to me if I called it. Nor a gorilla, see?'

'Well, *my* monkey won't come to you,' said Tinker, angrily. 'But what I've come to say is . . .'

Before he could finish his sentence, the man made a curious noise in his throat – rather like Mischief did when he was pleased about anything. Mischief looked at the man in surprised delight – and then leapt straight from Tinker's shoulder to his, nuzzling against his neck, making little crooning noises. Tinker was so amazed that he stared without saying a word.

'See?' said the man. 'He's my little friend already. Don't gawp so, little fellow. I've trained the monkey family all my life. You lend me this little chap and I'll teach him to ride a small tricycle in two days.'

'Come here, Mischief!' said Tinker, amazed and angry at the monkey's behaviour. But Mischief cuddled down still farther into the big man's neck. The man hauled him out and handed him to Tinker.

41

'There you are,' he said. 'Nice little fellow he is. What is it you wanted to say to me?'

'I've come to say that this field belongs to my father, Professor Hayling,' said Tinker. 'And you've no right to bring your caravans here. So please take them all out. My friends and I are planning to camp out here.'

'Well, I've no objection to that,' said the big man, good-temperedly. 'You choose your own corner, young man. If you don't interfere with us, we shan't interfere with you!'

A boy of about Tinker's age came sidling up, and looked at Tinker and Mischief with interest. 'Is he selling you that monkey, Grandad?' he asked.

'No I'm NOT!' almost shouted Tinker. 'I came to tell you and your caravans to clear out. This field belongs to my family.'

'Ah, but we've an old licence to come here every ten years, and show our circus,' said the bearded man. 'And believe it or not, there's been a Tapper's circus in this field every ten years since the year 1648. So you just run home and make no silly fuss, young man.'

'You're a fibber!' cried Tinker, losing his temper. 'I'll tell the police! I'll tell my father! I'll . . .'

'Don't you talk to my grandad like that!' shouted the boy, standing beside the old man. 'I'll hit you if you do!'

'I'll say what I like!' shouted Tinker, his temper now quite lost. 'And just you shut up!'

The very next moment Tinker found himself flat on his back on the grass. The boy had shot out his fist and hit Tinker hard in the chest! He struggled to his feet, red in the face, quite furious.

The old man fended him away. 'Don't you be silly now, boy,' he said. 'This youngster is a Tapper, like me, and he'll never give in. You go home and be sensible. We're not going to take notice of a hot-headed little kid like you. Our circus is coming in this here field, just like it has for years and years!'

He turned and walked to the nearest caravan. It was drawn by horses, and he clicked to them. They strained forward and the caravan followed. Others behind began to move too. The circus boy put his tongue out at Tinker. 'Sucks to you!' he said. 'Nobody gets the better of my grandad – or of me either! Still – it was plucky of you to go for him. I enjoyed it.'

'Shut up!' said Tinker, alarmed to find himself very near to tears. 'You just wait till my dad tells the police! You'll all go out much quicker than you came in – and one of these days I'll knock *you* down!'

He turned and ran back to the gate. He wondered what to do. He had so often heard his father say that the field behind their house belonged to him, and that he had let this or that farmer have the grazing rights for his horses and cattle. How DARE the travelling circus come into his father's field?

'I'll tell Dad,' he said to Anne, who was waiting at the gate. '*He* ought to turn them out! It's *our* field and I love it, especially just now when it's so green and beautiful, and the hedges are just going to be covered in white may. I'll tell Dad the boy knocked me down – shot out his fist just like *that* – and down I went. I'd like to do the same to *him*!'

He went into the house, followed by a puzzled Anne.

He looked into the sitting-room and saw George there.

'Tinker! That boy knocked you down!' said Anne, in a horrified voice. 'Why did he do that?'

'Oh – just because I told his grandad to take his caravans away,' said Tinker, feeling rather grand. 'He didn't hurt me at all – just punched me on the chest. Still – I said what I had gone to say.'

'But *will* they take the caravans away out of the field?' asked Anne.

'I told them I'd tell the police,' said Tinker. 'So I bet they'll skedaddle. They haven't any right to be there. It's *our* field!'

'*Are* you going to the police?' asked George, disbelievingly. 'I really don't see why you have to make such a fuss about it all, Tinker. They might make it difficult for *us* to go camping there.'

'But I tell you it's *my* field – Dad's always said so!' said Tinker. 'He said it wasn't any use to him, so I could consider it my own. And I do. AND we're going to camp in it, whatever anyone says! It's a travelling circus that's coming there, so the old man said.'

'Oh TINKER! How marvellous to have a circus at the bottom of the garden!' said George, her eyes shining, and Anne nodded too. Tinker glared at them.

'JUST like girls to say a thing like that!' he said. 'Would *you* want people trespassing all over a field that belonged to you, with horses neighing and tigers and lions roaring, and bears grunting, and chimpanzees stealing things – and

45

nasty circus boys being rude all the time, ready to knock you down?'

'Oh Tinker! You *do* make it sound so exciting!' said George. 'Will there really be lions and tigers? Suppose one escaped – what a thrill!'

'Well – *I* shouldn't like that,' said Anne, at once. 'I don't particularly want a lion peering in at my window, or a bear clomping round my bedroom!'

'Neither do I,' said Tinker, in a most decided voice. 'That's why I'm going to tell Dad about it. He's got the old document that sets out our rights to that field. He showed me it one day. I'll ask him about it, and if he'll let me see it, I'll take it straight to the police and let them turn out that rude old man and his horrible circus.'

'How do you *know* it's horrible?' asked George. 'It might be really good. I'm sure they'd let us camp in the corner nearest the garden, and we'd get a great view of what's going on all the time. Look – there's your father strolling down the path, smoking a pipe. He never does that if he's busy. It would be a good time to go and ask him about the document. He might even show it to us.'

'All right,' said Tinker, rather sulkily. 'But you'll see I'm right. Come on.'

However, Tinker proved to be quite, quite wrong! His father went to fetch the old, yellowed piece of parchment at once. 'Ha! Here it is!' he said. 'It's pretty valuable too, because it's so old. It dates back quite a few centuries.'

He undid the rather dirty piece of ribbon round it and unrolled it. Neither the girls nor Tinker could read the old-fashioned lettering.

'What does it all say?' asked Anne, with great interest.

'It says that the field known as "Cromwell's Corner" is to be held by the Hayling Family for always,' said Professor Hayling. 'It was given to them by Cromwell because our family allowed them to camp in that field when they sorely needed a rest after battle. It's been ours ever since.'

'So NOBODY else is allowed to camp in it, or use it for grazing or anything, unless we say so!' said Tinker, triumphantly.

'Quite right,' said his father. 'But wait a minute – I seem to remember an odd clause that said something about a travelling show – a show that had rights to camp in the field since about 1066. Not even Cromwell could alter that – it was in the original deeds, long before Cromwell battled in that district. Now let's see – that piece would come about the end, I expect.'

The two girls and Tinker waited while the Professor pored over the old and beautiful lettering. He jabbed his finger on to three lines towards the end.

'Yes. There it is. I'll quote it. Listen! "And let it be known that Ye Travelling Show so-named 'Tapper's Travelling Show', which has always had camping rights, shall still have the right to claim these once every ten years so long as the show travels the country ways – Given under my hand . . ." and so on and so on. Well – I don't expect that Tapper's Travelling Show is going now, all these years and years after the document was drawn up and signed in the year 1648. See – here's the date – if you can read the old figures!'

The children stared at the date, and then glanced up at Tinker. He looked angry and very red in the face. 'You might have told me all that before, Dad,' he said.

'Why?' asked his father, astonished. 'What possible interest can it have for you children?'

'Only that there's a circus called Tapper's Travelling Circus in that field this very minute,' said Anne. 'And the old man with it is called Tapper – and he said it was his right to be there, and . . .'

'He was rude to me and I want you to turn out this circus this very day!' said Tinker. '*We* want to camp there.'

'I'm sure Mr Tapper would have no objection to you camping there,' said his father. 'Aren't you being rather silly, Tinker? *You* weren't rude to any of the circus folk, were you?'

Tinker went very red, turned his back and stalked out of the room, Mischief clinging to his neck. He rubbed his chest where the circus boy had punched him. 'Just you wait!' he said in a whisper. 'I'll punch *you* one day!'

'Anne, if you and the others want to camp in the field, I'll go and speak to Mr Tapper,' said the Professor, puzzled by Tinker's behaviour.

'Oh no – it's all right,' said Anne, hastily. 'He has already said that it didn't matter if we camped there. Oh – there are the boys back again. I'll just go and see if they have brought back all our bicycles safely. Thank you for showing us that marvellous old document, Professor!'

And away she went looking rather hot and bothered!

CHAPTER SIX

Getting ready for camping out

DICK AND Julian were most interested to hear about Tinker and the travelling circus – and the old, old document.

'You made a bit of a fool of yourself,' said Julian, looking at Tinker. 'Still, there's no harm done, apparently. I vote we go and see where we can put up our tents. Personally, I shall be thrilled to see a bit of circus life so close to me! I wonder how they'll manage to put on a show. I suppose they've everything with them, and can put up a circus ring and a tent and anything else necessary.'

'There are a lot of big vans,' said Anne. 'I went down to have a look about half an hour ago. The field is almost full now, except for one corner near our hedge that I suppose they have left for our tents.'

'I saw the posters about the circus as we cycled back,' said Dick. 'Dead-Shot Dick – Chimpanzee that plays Cricket – the Boneless Man – Madelon and her Beautiful Horses – Monty and Winks, the Clowns – the Dancing Donkey – Mr Wooh, the Wonder Wizard – gosh, it sounded *quite* a circus. I'm glad we can camp in the same field – we shall really see behind the scenes, then.'

GETTING READY FOR CAMPING OUT

'Don't forget there was Charlie the Chimp, and the Bonzo Band,' said Julian. 'What fun if the chimp got loose and peeped in at the kitchen window!'

'It wouldn't be at *all* funny,' said Anne. 'Jenny would run for miles! So would Tinker's monkey!'

'What about putting up our own tents after tea?' said Dick. 'Jim said he'd have them here by tea time. It's hotter than ever today. I don't feel I can do much at the moment. I just want to laze.'

'Woof,' said Timmy, who was lying down with his head on his paws, panting.

'You feel the same, old chap, don't you?' said Julian, poking him with his toe. 'You're tired out with your long run back from Kirrin, aren't you?'

'The roads were so *dusty*!' said Dick. 'He kept sneezing whenever a car passed us, because the dust got up his nose. Poor old Tim. You really are tired out with that long, long run!'

'Woof!' said Tim, suddenly sitting up straight and pawing vigorously at George. Everyone laughed.

'He says he's not at *all* tired, he wants a walk,' chuckled Dick.

'Well, if he's not tired, I *am*,' said Julian. 'It really was a job sorting out all our things at Kirrin – and cycling all the way back. NO, Timmy – I am NOT going to take you for a walk!'

Timmy whined, and at once Mischief the monkey leapt down from Tinker's shoulder and went to cuddle against the big dog, making small comforting noises. He even put his thin little arms round Timmy's neck!

'You're being just a *little* soppy, Mischief,' said Tinker, but Mischief didn't care. His big friend was sad about something, or he wouldn't have whined. Timmy put out a big red tongue and licked the little creature delicately on his nose. Then he suddenly pricked up his ears, and sat straight up. He had heard a noise from somewhere. So had all the others.

'It's music of some kind,' said Anne. 'Oh – I believe I know what it is!'

'What?' said the others.

'It must be Tapper's Travelling Circus Band practising for opening night,' said Anne.

'Well, that's tomorrow,' yawned George. 'Yes – it does sound like a band. Maybe we shall see the bandsmen after tea, when we put up our tents. I'd like to see the Boneless Man, wouldn't you?'

'NO!' said Anne. 'He'd be all limp and wriggly and horrid – like a worm or a jellyfish! I shan't go and see him. But I'd love to see the horses and the Dancing Donkey. Does he dance to the band, do you think?'

'We'll find out when we go,' said Dick, 'as it opens tomorrow. If Mr Tapper isn't annoyed about Tinker trying to turn them out, he might let us wander round.'

'I don't think I want to come,' said Tinker. 'Mr Tapper was rude – and that boy knocked me flat.'

'Well, I expect I'd do the same if I thought you were

being rude to *my* grandad,' said Julian, lazily. 'Now – it's settled, is it, that we go down with our things to the field after tea, and see if we can put up our tents in some sheltered corner?'

'Yes,' said everyone. Dick idly tickled Mischief's nose with a thin blade of grass. The monkey sneezed at once, and then again. He rubbed his little paw across his nose and stared disapprovingly at Dick. Then he sneezed once more.

'Borrow a hanky, old thing,' said Julian. And, to everyone's intense amusement, Mischief leapt across to Dick and neatly pulled his handkerchief out of his pocket! Then he pretended to blow his nose.

Everyone roared with laughter, and Mischief was delighted. 'You'll be stolen to act in a circus one day, if you behave like that!' said Dick, snatching back his hanky. 'The Pickpocket Monkey!'

'He'd be very good in a circus,' said Julian.

'I'd *never* let him join a circus!' said Tinker at once. 'He might have a dreadful life.'

'No. I don't think he would,' said Julian. 'Circus folk love their animals and are proud of them. And after all, if they treated them unkindly, the animals wouldn't be happy or healthy, and couldn't enjoy their acts. *Most* circus people treat their animals like one of the family.'

'What! Even a chimpanzee!' said Anne, in horror.

'They're nice creatures – and very clever,' said Julian. 'Mischief, do *not* remove my handkerchief, please. It was

53

funny the first time, but *not* a second time. Look at him now, trying to undo Timmy's collar.'

'Come and sit quietly by me, Mischief,' ordered Tinker, and the little creature obediently went to him and cuddled on to his knee, making a soft, crooning noise.

'You're a humbug,' said Tinker, fondling him. 'You be careful I don't give you away to the circus, and get an elephant in exchange!'

'Idiot!' said Dick, and everyone laughed at the thought of Tinker and an elephant. What in the world would he do with it?

A voice called from the house. 'Tinker! Jim's here with all the camping things. He's put them in the hall, *just* where your father will fall over them. You'd better come and see to them now.'

'In a few minutes, Jenny!' called back Tinker. 'We're busy.'

'You're a real fibber, Tinker,' said Dick. 'We are *not* busy. You could easily go to find out where the things are, and see if they're all there. There are quite a lot.'

'We'll go in twenty minutes or so,' said Anne, yawning. 'I bet Tinker's father is asleep this hot afternoon. He won't stir out of his study.'

But she was wrong. Professor Hayling was wide awake, and when he had finished his work, he wanted a drink of very cold water. He threw open his study door, strode out towards the kitchen – and fell over a pile of all kinds of camping gear, bringing them down with a tremendous noise.

FIVE ARE TOGETHER AGAIN

Jenny rushed out of the kitchen with loud screams of fright, and the Professor bellowed in anger as he took a ground-sheet off his head, and a tent-pole off his back. 'WHAT ARE THESE THINGS? I WILL NOT HAVE THEM IN THE HALL! JENNY! JENNY! Take them down to the bonfire and burn the lot!'

'Our camping things!' cried George, listening in horror. 'Quick! We must get them! Oh, I do hope Tinker's father hasn't hurt himself. Bother, bother, bother!'

While Julian and Dick deftly removed everything that had fallen on to the angry Professor and took it all down the garden, Anne and George comforted him, and made such a fuss of him that he began to feel decidedly less angry. He sat down in a chair and wiped his forehead. 'I hope you've taken all those things down to the bottom of the garden,' he said after a while.

'Yes,' said Tinker, truthfully. 'Er – they're all by the bonfire, but it's not lit yet.'

'I light it myself tomorrow,' said his father, and Tinker heaved a sigh of relief. His father would forget, of course – and anyhow, everything was going to be taken into the camping field after tea.

'Have a cup of nice hot tea,' said Jenny, appearing with a tray of tea things. 'Sit down and drink this. It's newly made. Best thing to have after a fall and a shock.'

She turned and whispered crossly to Tinker, 'Didn't I call to you and tell you the Professor would trip over those things, the poor man? Now you just get your own tea, while I take him into the dining-room and comfort him with a nice hot scone, and a cup of tea!'

'I'll get *our* tea,' said Anne. 'Then we'll set up the tents down in the field, and enjoy ourselves. And Tinker, don't you get into any more trouble with the circus folk.'

'I'll see he doesn't,' said George, firmly. 'Come on – let's go down to the field while Anne gets the tea. I could do with a bun or two!'

Between them, Dick and Julian had lugged all the things down the garden – two tents, ground-sheets, blankets, tent-pegs and all the rest. Timmy ran with them in excitement, wondering what all the fuss was about. Mischief, of course, leapt to the top of whatever was being carried, and chattered excitedly all the way down the garden.

He got into trouble when he ran off with a tent-peg, but Timmy managed to catch him and make him drop it. Then, very solemnly, Timmy carried the tent-peg to Julian.

'Good dog!' said Julian. 'Just keep an eye on that wicked little monkey, Tim, will you? There are all sorts of things he might run off with!'

So Timmy kept an eye on Mischief, nosing him away whenever he thought the monkey was going to pick up something he shouldn't. Finally Mischief became tired of Timmy's nose and leapt on his back, where, clinging to the dog's collar, he rode just as if he were on horseback. 'Only it's dogback, not horseback,' said George, with a laugh.

'They would make quite a good pair for the circus,' said Dick. 'I bet Mischief could hold on to reins, if Timmy had any!'

'Well, he's not *going* to have any,' said George. 'The next thing would be a whip! Whew! What a lot of things we've got – is that the lot?'

It was, thank goodness. A bell rang out from the house at that moment, and everyone heaved a sigh of relief.

'Tea at last!' said Dick. 'I could drink a whole potful. Come on – we've finished piling up all the things. We'll get busy after tea with them, I can't do a thing more. Don't you agree, Timmy?'

'WOOF!' said Timmy, heartily, and galloped up the

garden path at top speed, with Mischief scampering after him.

'Talk about a circus!' said Dick. 'We've a ready-made one here! All right, Anne – we're coming! We're coming!'

CHAPTER SEVEN

In the circus field

NOBODY WANTED to spend a long time over tea. They all longed to go down to the field and set up their little camp.

'We shall have a wonderful look-in at what goes on in a circus camp,' said Dick. 'We shall be living so near the circus folk! I do hope Mischief won't get too friendly with the people there. They might take him away with them when they leave.'

'*Indeed* they won't!' said Tinker, fiercely. 'What a thing to say! As if Mischief would go with them, anyhow! I don't expect he'll mix with the circus crowd at all.'

'You wait and see!' grinned Dick. 'Now buck up with your tea – I'm longing to go and set our camp in the field, and see what's going on there.'

It wasn't long before they were ready. They were soon down by the fence, and gazed over it in amazement. Great vans were in the field, all with Mr Tapper's name on and all painted in bright colours. There were caravans too, much smaller than the great vans, and these had windows, each with neat lace curtains. The circus folk lived in the caravans, of course, and George found herself wishing that she herself could go about in one, instead of living in a house that couldn't move anywhere!

'Look at the horses!' cried Dick, as a bunch of them appeared with tossing heads and beautiful long thick tails. The boy who had knocked Tinker down was with them, whistling. They were all coming from a big horse-van, and were delighted to be in a field with lush green grass.

'Is that gate properly shut?' yelled an enormous voice, and the boy yelled back, 'Yes, Grandad. I shut it. There's nowhere the horses can get out. Don't they like this grass!'

Then he saw Julian and the others all looking over the fence, and waved to them. 'See our horses? Aren't they a great lot?'

And, just to show off a little, he leapt on to the back of the nearest one, and went all round the edge of the field with it. George watched him enviously. If only *she* could have a horse like that!

'Well, let's take our camp things into the field,' said Tinker. 'The nearer we are to the circus the better. We ought to have some fun.'

He climbed over the fence and Dick followed. 'I'll hand everything over,' said Julian. 'George can help me – she's a strong old thing!'

George grinned. She loved to hear anyone say that! It was quite a job getting some of the things over the fence. The tents, neatly wrapped though they were, were heavy, awkward things to handle, but at last everything was safely over, lying on the grass.

Then Julian, Anne and George climbed over the fence too, and stood in the field, looking round for a good corner to set up their things.

'What about near those bushes over there?' said Julian. 'There's that big tree behind as well to protect us from the wind – and we aren't *too* near the circus folk – they might not like us right on top of them – and yet we're near enough to see what's going on.'

'Oh, it's going to be Fun!' said Anne, her eyes shining.

'I think I'd better go and find the old grandad – Mr Tapper,' said Julian. 'Just to tell him we're here, in case he thinks we're intruders and have no right to be here.'

'You haven't got to ask his permission for us to be in MY field!' said Tinker, at once.

'Now don't keep flying off the handle like that, Tinker,' said Julian. 'This is merely a question of good manners – something you don't seem to know much about! How do we know that the circus folk won't resent us camping so near them? Much better to show ourselves friendly from the start.'

'All right, all right,' said Tinker, sulkily. 'But it is *my* field, after all! You'll be telling me to be friends with that nasty circus boy next!'

'Well, you'd better be – else he might knock you flat again!' said George. 'Anyway, be sensible, Tinker – it's not often people have a circus just at the bottom of their garden, and can pop over the fence and mix with the circus folk.'

Julian walked over to the nearest caravan. It was empty – no one answered his knock.

'What you want, mister?' called a high little voice, and a small girl with tangled, untidy hair came running up:

'Where's Mr Tapper?' asked Julian, smiling at the bright-eyed little thing.

'He's with one of the horses,' said the small girl. 'Who are you?'

'We're your neighbours,' said Julian. 'Will you take us to Mr Tapper?'

'Old Grandad's this way,' said the child, and slipped a dirty little hand into Julian's. 'I'll show you. I like you.'

She led the children to the middle of the camp. A mournful howl came from somewhere behind them and George stopped suddenly. 'That's Timmy! He must have found out that we've got out of the garden. I'll go back for him.'

'Better not,' said Julian. 'There might be ructions if he met the chimpanzee. A big chimp would make mincemeat of him!'

'It *wouldn't*!' said George, but all the same she didn't go back to fetch Timmy. Julian hoped that the dog wouldn't jump over the fence and come to find them.

'There's old Grandad Tapper on those steps,' said the

little girl, smiling up at Julian, whose hand she still held. 'I like you, mister.' Then she shouted loudly to the old fellow sitting on the steps of a nearby caravan. 'Grandad! Here's folks to see you!'

Grandad was looking at a beautiful chestnut-brown horse, tethered close to him. He had one of the horse's hooves in his hand. The children stood and gazed at him – black beard, frowning eyebrows – and, oh dear! thought Anne, only one ear, poor man. What *could* have happened to the missing one?

'GRANDAD!' called the girl again. 'SOME FOLKS TO SEE YOU!'

Mr Tapper looked round, his eyes very bright under his black eyebrows. He set the horse's hoof down, and gave the lovely creature a pat. 'You don't need to limp any more, my beauty,' he said. 'I've taken out the stone that was in your hoof. You can dance again!'

The horse lifted up its magnificent head and neighed as if it were saying thank you. Tinker almost jumped out of his skin, and Mischief slipped from his shoulder and cuddled under his arm in terror.

'Now, now, little monkey, don't you know a horse's voice when you hear one?' said Grandad, and Mischief poked his head out from under Tinker's arm to listen.

'Does that horse *really* dance?' said Anne, longing to stroke its long, smooth nose.

FIVE ARE TOGETHER AGAIN

'Dance! It's one of the finest dancing horses in the world!' said Grandad, and began to whistle a lively little tune. The horse pricked up its ears, gazed at Grandad, and then began to dance! The children watched in astonishment.

There it went, round and round, nodding its head to the tune, its feet tapping the grass in perfect time to Grandad's whistling.

'Oh, the lovely thing!' said George. 'Do *all* your horses dance as well as this one?'

'Yes. Some a good deal better,' said Grandad. 'This one has a fair ear for music, but not as good an ear as some. You wait till you see them dressed up, with feathery plumes nodding on their heads. Horses – there's nothing in the world as beautiful as a good horse.'

'Mr Tapper – we come from the house over the fence there,' said Julian, feeling that it was time to explain their visit. 'As you probably know, Tinker's father owns this field, and . . .'

'Yes, yes – but we have an old right to come every so often,' said the old man, raising his voice. 'Now don't you start arg . . .'

'I haven't come to argue with you,' said Julian, politely. 'I've only just come to say that we – that is my friends here and I – would like to come and camp in this field, but we shouldn't annoy you in any way, and . . .'

'Oh well – if that's what you want, you're more than welcome!' said the old man. 'More than welcome! I thought maybe you'd think you could turn us out – like that youngster there would like to do!' And he nodded at Tinker.

Tinker went red and said nothing. The old man laughed. 'Ha! My grandson didn't think much of that idea, did he, youngster? He hit out, and down you went on your back. He's got a temper, he has, young Jeremy. But another time maybe he'll find himself on *his* back, eh?'

'Yes. He will,' said Tinker, at once.

'Right. Well, you'll be even with one another then, and you can shake hands like gentlemen,' said the old man, his eyes twinkling. 'Now – what about you bringing your gear right into the field, and setting up your tents? I'll get old Charlie the Chimp to help you. He's as strong as ten men!'

'The *chimpanzee*! Is he tame enough to help us to put up our *tents*?' said Anne, disbelievingly.

'Old Charlie is cleverer than all of you put together, and as tame as you are!' said Grandad. 'And he could beat you three boys at cricket any day! You bring your bat along one morning and watch him. I'll call him to help you. CHARLIE! CHARLIE! Where are you? Snoozing I suppose!'

But no Charlie came. 'You go and fetch him,' said the old man, pointing to a corner of the field where stood a big, strong cage, with a tarpaulin roof to keep out the rain. 'He'll do anything you want him to do, so long as you give him a word of praise now and again!'

FIVE ARE TOGETHER AGAIN

'Let's get him, Ju,' said Dick, eagerly. 'Fancy having a chimpanzee to help us!'

And off they all went to the great cage. CHARLIE! CHARLIE! Wake up, you're wanted! CHARLIE!

CHAPTER EIGHT

Charlie the Chimp is a help!

TINKER CAME to the big cage first. He peered inside. Charlie the Chimp was there all right, sitting at the back of his cage, his brown eyes looking at the children with curiosity. He got up and went over to where Tinker was peering in and pressed his nose against the strong wire, almost against Tinker's. Then he blew hard and Tinker backed away, surprised and cross.

'He *blew* at me!' he said to the others, who were laughing at Tinker's disgust. The chimp made a funny noise that Mischief the monkey immediately tried to imitate. The chimpanzee stared at Mischief, then he grew very excited. He rattled his cage, jumped up and down, and made some very odd noises indeed.

A boy came running up at once. It was the boy who had knocked Tinker down. 'Hey – what are you doing to the chimp?' he called. 'Oh – aren't you the boy who shouted at my grandad – the one I knocked down?'

'Yes. And don't you dare try that on again, or you'll be sorry!' said Tinker in a fierce voice.

'Shut up, Tinker,' said Julian. He turned to the boy. 'Your name's Jeremy, isn't it?' he said. 'Well, we've just been talking to your grandad over there, and he said we could get the chimpanzee to help us with our camping gear. It's all right for him to come out of his cage, isn't it?'

'Oh yes – I take him out two or three times a day,' said Jeremy. 'He gets bored in his cage. He'd love to help put up your tents – he's always helping us with things like that. He's as strong as a lion.'

'Is he – er – is he safe?' asked Dick, eyeing the big animal doubtfully.

'Safe? What do you mean – safe?' asked Jeremy, surprised. 'He's as safe as I am! Charlie, come on out! Go on, you can undo your cage perfectly well, you know you can!'

The chimpanzee made a funny little chuckling noise, put his hand through the wire, reached the bolt, pulled it, took his hand back – and pushed open the cage door.

'See! Easy, isn't it?' said Jeremy, grinning. 'Charlie boy, come along. Your help's wanted!'

Charlie lumbered out of his cage, and went with the children to where they had left their tents and groundsheets and the rest. He walked with his fists on the ground in a most inelegant manner, making a funny little groaning noise all the time. Mischief was rather afraid of him, and kept well to the back – but the chimpanzee suddenly turned round, caught hold of Mischief, and sat him up on his shoulder! Mischief held on, not knowing whether to be scared or jubilant!

'I wish I had my camera here,' said Anne to George. 'Just look at them – Mischief is as pleased as can be!'

They arrived at the pile of camping gear. 'Carry this, Charlie, and follow us,' ordered Jeremy. The chimp grabbed at this, that and the other, and, with his great arms full, followed the children to where they thought they could camp, with the great tree to shelter them from the wind.

'Drop those things, Charlie,' said Jeremy, 'and go back for the rest. Buck up. Don't stand there staring! You've got work to do!'

But Charlie still crouched there, staring straight at Mischief. 'Oh! He wants Mischief the monkey to go with him!' cried George. 'Go on, Mischief, have a ride again!'

Mischief leapt up on to the chimpanzee's shoulders. Charlie put up a great paw to steady him and then lumbered off to fetch the rest of the things. One of the ground-sheets came undone and slithered over his head like a tent, so that he couldn't see where he was going. In a rage he leapt on it and began to jump up and down, up and down, growling most terrifyingly. The children felt rather scared.

'Charlie, don't be silly!' said Jeremy, and pulled it away from him, rolling it up swiftly. The chimpanzee could manage it then, and his good temper immediately came back again.

Everything was soon piled up in one place, and Julian and Dick began to put up the tents. Charlie watched them with the greatest interest, and helped most intelligently when he saw that he could.

'He's a good sort, isn't he?' said Jeremy, proud that his friend the chimpanzee could show off like this. 'Did you see him put that tent-pole in exactly the right place? And you ought to see him fetch the pails of water for the horses each day. He carries a full pail in each hand!'

72

CHARLIE THE CHIMP IS A HELP!

'He ought to get wages,' said Tinker.

'He does!' said Jeremy. 'He gets eight bananas a day and as many oranges as he likes. And he LOVES sweets!'

'Oh! I think I've got some!' said Tinker and delved into one of his pockets. He brought up a peculiar mixture of things, among which was a screwed-up sweet bag. Inside was a mass of half-melted boiled sweets.

'You can't give him *those*!' said Anne. 'They're old and sticky and messy!'

But Charlie thought differently. He took the paper bag straight out of Tinker's hand, sniffed it – and then put the whole thing into his mouth at once!

'He'll choke!' said Julian.

'Not Charlie!' said Jeremy. 'Let him be. He'll go straight back to his cage, get in, shoot the bolt and sit there sucking sweets till they're gone. He'll be as happy as can be.'

'Well – he certainly deserved a reward,' said George. 'He did all the heavy work! Come on, let's finish putting everything straight. Hey – won't it be fun sleeping out in tents tonight! We'd better have supper first.'

'You can come and join *us*, if you like,' said Jeremy. 'We don't have posh food like you, of course – but it's good food, all the same. Old Grandma cooks it in her pot. She's two hundred years old.'

The children laughed in disbelief. 'Two hundred! Nobody lives as long as that!' said George.

'Well, that's what she tells everyone,' said Jeremy. 'And

she looks it, too! But her eyes are as sharp as needles still! Shall I tell her you'll be here to supper?'

'Well – would there be enough for so many extra?' said Julian. 'We meant to bring our own meal. Should we bring that and share everything with you? We've more than enough. Jenny said she would have it all ready for us to bring down tonight – a meat pie, cold sausages, and apples and bananas.'

'Sh! Don't say bananas in front of Charlie,' said Jeremy. 'He'll worry you for them all the time. All right – you bring your food and we'll share with you round our camp-fire. I'll tell old Grandma. We're having a sing-song tonight, and Fred the Fiddler's playing his fiddle. Ah, that fiddle! Its tunes get into your feet and away you go!'

This all sounded very exciting. Julian thought they ought to go back home before anyone began to be worried about their complete disappearance, and pack up the food for supper that night.

'We'll be back as soon as we can,' said he. 'And thanks a lot for all your help. Come on, Mischief. Say goodbye to Charlie for the moment, and don't look so gloomy. We're coming back here tonight!'

They all went back over the fence, feeling a little tired now, but full of their plans for the evening. 'It's almost like *belonging* to the circus, going back to sit round a camp fire and eat supper from that old black stewpot on the fire,' said Tinker. 'I bet the supper will taste delicious. I hope Dad won't mind us popping off to the circus camp.'

'I don't expect he'll even notice that we've gone,' said

George. 'My father never notices things like that. Sometimes he doesn't even notice when people are there, in
front of his nose!'

'Well, that must be useful at times if they're people he
doesn't like,' said Tinker. 'Now – let's see what Jenny's got
that we can take back with us.'

Jenny listened wide-eyed to all they had to say. 'Well,
well, well!' she said. 'Camping out with the circus folk!
Whatever next? I'd like to know what your parents would
think of *that*!'

'We'll ask them, next time we see them,' said Julian,
with a grin. 'What do you have for our supper? We're
taking it down to our camp.'

'I thought maybe you'd do that,' said Jenny. 'It's all cold. A meat pie, cold sausages, a cucumber and lettuce hearts and tomatoes, rolls, and apples and bananas. Will that be enough?'

'Gosh, yes,' said Tinker, thrilled. 'What about something to drink?'

'You can take lemonade or orangeade with you, whichever you like,' said Jenny. 'But listen now – don't go bursting into your father's workroom. He's worked hard all day, and he's tired.'

'And cross, I expect,' said Tinker. 'People are always cross when they're tired. Except you, dear, dear Jenny.'

'Ha! You want something else out of my cupboard, calling me your dear, dear Jenny,' she said with a twinkle.

'Could we have some sugar lumps?' asked Tinker. 'Oh, Jenny, there are the loveliest horses you ever saw down in the circus field. I want to give them a sugar lump each.'

'And yourself a few as well!' said Jenny. 'All right. I'll pack up everything for you, and give you a few enamel plates and mugs and knives. What about Timmy? Doesn't he want a meal too?'

'Wuff!' said Timmy, glad that someone had remembered him. Jenny patted his big head. 'It's all ready in the larder for you,' she said. 'George, you go and get it. He must be hungry.'

George fetched a plate of meat and biscuits from the larder and Timmy fell on it with happy little barks. Yes – he was very, VERY hungry!

CHARLIE THE CHIMP IS A HELP!

At last all the food was ready, packed to take down the garden to the field. What a lot there seemed! Well, they would certainly have plenty to spare for their circus friends. They said good night to Jenny, and set off down the garden again. They thought they had better not disturb Professor Hayling.

'He might be cross and forbid us to go and eat with the circus folk,' said Tinker. 'Mischief, come off that basket, and don't pretend you weren't fishing in it for a banana. And please put on your best table manners tonight, or Charlie the Chimp will be ashamed of you!'

It was fun going back down the garden and over the fence into the field again. The sun was sinking fast and soon the shadows would fall. How lovely to sit round a fire and eat supper with the kindly circus folk – and perhaps to sing old songs with them – and hear Fred the Fiddler fiddle his old, old tunes! What fun to creep into a tent, and sleep with the cries of owls around, and stars shining in at the tent opening!

There they go, over the fence, handing the food one to another. Take your paw out of that basket, Mischief! That's right, Timmy, nibble his ear if he's as mischievous as his name! You're all going to have some fun tonight!

CHAPTER NINE

A wonderful evening

As SOON as Jeremy saw the visitors climbing over the fence, he ran to help them. He was very excited at the thought of having guests. He took them over to old Grandad first, to be welcomed.

'Now I expect your friends will like to see round a bit,' said Grandad. 'Charlie the Chimp can go with you. We've a rehearsal on tonight, so the ring has been set up. You can watch some of the show.'

This was great news. The children saw that curved pieces of painted wood had been set together to make a great ring in the field, and as they went across the grass, the Musical Horses began to troop into the ring, the leading one ridden by Madelon, a lovely girl dressed in shimmering gold.

How beautiful they are! thought Anne, as she watched. Look at their great feathery plumes, nodding on their magnificent heads.

The Bonzo Band struck up just then, and the horses at once trotted in perfect time to the music. The band looked a little peculiar as the bandsmen had not put on their smart uniforms. They were saving those for the opening night!

78

A WONDERFUL EVENING

The horses trotted prettily out of the ring after two or three rounds, the beautiful Madelon on the leading horse. Then in came Fred the Fiddler and played his violin for a few minutes. First the music was slow and solemn, then Fred began to play quickly, and the children found themselves jigging about, up and down and round about. 'I can't keep still!' panted Anne. 'The tune's got into my feet.'

Charlie the Chimp came up just then, walking on hind legs, and looking unexpectedly tall. He usually walked on all fours. He began to jig about too, looking very funny. He ran right into the ring and put his arms round Fred the Fiddler's legs. 'He loves Fred,' said Jeremy. 'Now he's going to rehearse his cricket act. I must go and bowl to him.'

And off went Jeremy into the ring. The chimpanzee rushed over to him and hugged him. A bat was thrown into the ring, and Charlie picked it up and made a few swipes into the air with it, making delighted noises all the time.

Then a cricket ball was thrown to Jeremy, who caught it deftly. A small girl appeared from somewhere and set up three stumps for a wicket. 'Can't find the bails, Jeremy!' she called. 'Have you got them in your pocket?'

'No,' said Jeremy. 'Never mind, I'll knock the stumps right over!'

But that wasn't so easy with Charlie the Chimp at the wicket! He took a terrific swipe at the ball and it went right over Jeremy's head, too high to catch. The chimp lost his balance and sat down on the wicket, knocking the stumps out of the ground.

'OUT!' yelled Jeremy, but the chimp wasn't having that. He carefully put up the stumps again, and then set himself in front once more, waggling the bat.

It was the funniest cricket that the children had ever seen! The chimpanzee was very, very clever with the bat, and sent poor Jeremy running all over the place. Then he chased the boy all round the ring with the bat, making curious chortling noises. The children didn't know if he was amused or angry! Finally he threw the bat at Jeremy and walked off, scratching himself under one arm.

FIVE ARE TOGETHER AGAIN

The children roared with laughter at him. 'He's as good as any clown!' said Dick. 'Jeremy, does he do this cricket act every night when the circus is open?'

'Oh yes – and sometimes he hits the ball into the audience,' said Jeremy. 'There's great excitement then. Sometimes, for a treat, we let one of the boys in the audience come down and bowl to Charlie. One bowled him right out once, and Charlie was so cross that he chased him all round the ring three times – just as he chased *me* just now. The boy didn't like it much!'

Charlie came up to Jeremy and put his great arms round him, trying to swing him off the ground. 'Stop that, Charlie,' said Jeremy, wriggling free. 'Look out – here comes the Dancing Donkey! Better get out of the ring – goodness knows what antics *he'll* be up to!'

In came the Dancing Donkey. He was dark grey, and tossed his head as he came galloping in. He stood and looked round at everyone. Then he sat down, lifted up a leg and scratched his nose. The children stared in astonishment. They had never in their lives seen a donkey do *that* before! Then, when the band suddenly began to play, the donkey stood up and listened, flapping his ears first one way and then another, and nodding his head in time to the music.

The band changed its tune to a march. The donkey listened again, and then began to march round the ring in perfect time – clip-clop-clip-clop-clip-clop. Then it apparently felt tired, and sat down heavily on its back legs. The children couldn't help laughing. The donkey got up, and somehow its back legs became entangled with its front ones and it fell down, looking most ridiculous.

'Has it hurt itself?' asked Anne, anxiously. 'Oh dear – it will break one of its legs if it goes on like this. Look, it can't untangle them, Jeremy.'

The donkey gave a mournful bray, tried to get up, and flopped down again. The band changed its tune, and the donkey leapt up at once, and began to do a kind of tap dance – clickety-click, clickety-click, clickety-click – it was marvellous!

'I shouldn't have thought that a donkey could possibly have been taught to tap dance,' said George.

Soon the donkey seemed to feel tired again. It stopped dancing, but the band still went on playing. The donkey ran towards it and stamped a foot.

A weird voice suddenly came from it. 'Too fast! TOO FAST!' But the band took no notice and went on playing. The donkey bent down, wriggled hard – and its head fell off on to the grass in the ring! Anne gave a shriek of fright.

'Don't be an idiot, Anne,' said Dick. 'You didn't think the donkey was a *real* one, did you?'

'*Isn't* it?' said Anne, relieved. 'It looks *just* like that donkey that used to give rides to children on Kirrin beach.'

The donkey now split in half and a small man climbed

out of each half, both taking their legs carefully out of the donkey's legs. The donkey-skin fell to the ground and lay there, flat and collapsed.

'Wish *I* had a donkey-skin like that,' said Tinker. 'I've got a friend at school who could be the back legs and I'd be the front legs. The things we'd do!'

'Well, I must say you'd make a first-class donkey, the way you behave sometimes,' said George. 'Look, this must be Dead-Shot Dick coming on.'

But before Dead-Shot Dick could do any of his shooting tricks, the two donkey-men had run to the band and begun a loud argument with them.

'Why play so fast? You *know* we can't do our tricks at top speed. Are you trying to mess up our turn?'

The bandleader shouted something back. It must have been rude, because one of the donkey-men shook his fist and began to run towards the band.

A loud voice crashed in on the argument and made everyone jump. It was Mr Tapper, old Grandad, giving his orders in an enormous voice.

'ENOUGH! You, Pat, and you, Jim, get out of the ring. I give the orders, not you. ENOUGH, I SAY!'

The two donkey-men glared at him, but did not dare to say a word more. They stalked out of the ring, taking the donkey-skin with them.

Dead-Shot Dick looked very ordinary, dressed in a rather untidy flannel suit. 'He's not going to go all through his act,' said Jeremy. 'You'll see him another night, when the show's on for the public – he shoots at all kinds of things – even a five-pence piece dangling on a long string from the roof – and never misses! He's got a smashing rig-out too – sequins sewn all over his trousers and jersey – and his little horse is a wonder – goes round and round the ring and never turns a hair when Dead-Shot Dick fires his gun! Look – there he is, peeping in to see if Dick's coming back to him.'

A small white horse was looking anxiously at the ring, its eyes fixed on Dead-Shot Dick. It pawed the ground as if to say 'Buck up! I'm waiting for you! Am I to come on or not?'

'All right, Dick – you can go off now,' shouted Grand-ad. 'I hear your horse has hurt a foot – give him a good rest tonight. We'll want him on tomorrow.'

'Right, sir!' said Dead-Shot Dick. He saluted smartly, and ran off to his little horse.

'What's next, Jeremy?' asked George, who was enjoying everything very much.

'Don't know. Let's see – there's the acrobats – but the trapeze-swings aren't put up yet, so they won't come on tonight. And there's the Boneless Man – look, there he is. Good old Boney! I like him. He's free with his money, he is, not like some of the other folk!'

The Boneless Man looked very peculiar. He was re-markably thin, and remarkably tall. He walked in, looking quite extraordinary. 'He can't be boneless!' said Dick. 'He couldn't walk if he was!'

But the Boneless Man soon began to seem absolutely boneless. His legs gave way at the knees, and his ankles turned over so that he sank down to the ground, unable to walk. He could bend his arms all kinds of different ways, and turned his head almost completely round on his neck. He did a few peculiar things with his apparently boneless body, and finally wriggled along the ground exactly like a snake!

'He'll be dressed in a sort of snake-skin when he does his act properly,' said Jeremy. 'Funny, isn't he?'

'How on earth does he do it?' wondered Julian amazed. 'He bends his arms and legs all the wrong ways! Mine would break if I did that!'

A WONDERFUL EVENING

'Oh, it's easy for *him*!' said Jeremy. 'It's just that he's completely double-jointed – he can bend his arms both ways, and his legs both ways, and make them seem so loose that it looks as if he really *is* boneless. He's a nice chap. You'd like him.'

Anne felt a bit doubtful. What strange people made up a circus! It was a world of its own. She jumped suddenly as there came the sound of a trumpet blowing loudly.

'That's for supper,' said Jeremy, gleefully. 'Come on – let's go to old Grandma and her pot! Buck up, all of you!'

CHAPTER TEN

Round the camp fire

JEREMY LED the way out of the circus ring. It had been well-lit, and the night seemed very dark outside the ring. They went over the field to where a large fire was burning, cleverly set about with stones. An enormous cooking pot was hung over it, and a very, very nice smell came to their noses as they went near.

Old Grandma was there, of course, and she began stirring the pot when she saw them. 'You've been a long time in the ring,' she grumbled to Grandad. 'Anything gone wrong?'

'No,' said Grandad, and sniffed the air. 'I'm hungry. That smells good. Jeremy, help your grandma.'

'Yes, Grandad,' said Jeremy, and took a pile of plates to the old lady, who at once began ladling out pieces of meat and potatoes and vegetables from the steaming pot. Old Grandad turned to Julian.

'Well – did you like our little rehearsal?' he asked.

'Oh *yes*!' said Julian. 'I'm only sorry you didn't rehearse *all* the turns. I badly wanted to see the acrobats and the clowns. Are they here? I can't see them.'

'Oh yes – there's one clown over there – look – with Madelon, who had the horses,' said Grandad.

ROUND THE CAMP FIRE

The children looked – and were very disappointed. 'Is he a *clown*?' said Dick, disbelievingly. 'He doesn't look a bit funny. He looks miserable.'

'That's Monty all right,' said Grandad. 'He always looks like that out of the ring. He'll make you double up with laughter when the circus is on, he's a born clown – but a lot of clowns are like Monty when they're not performing – not much to say for themselves, and looking miserable. Winks is a bit livelier – that's him, pulling Madelon's hair. He'll get a smacked face in a minute, he's a real tease. There – I knew he'd get a clip on the ear!'

Winks went howling over to the children, boohooing most realistically. 'She smacked me!' he said. 'And she's got such p-p-p-pretty hair!'

The children couldn't help laughing. Mischief ran to the clown, jumped up on his shoulder and chattered comforting monkey words into his ear. Charlie the Chimp let himself out of his cage, and came to put his great paw into Winks' hand. They both thought that Winks really was hurt.

'That's enough, Winks,' said Grandad. 'You'll have the horses comforting you next! You do that in the ring tomorrow when we open, and you'll bring the house down. Sit down and have your supper.'

'Mr Tapper,' said Julian. 'There's another member of your circus we didn't see at the rehearsal – and that's Mr Wooh, the Wonder Magician. Why wasn't he there?'

'Oh, he never rehearses,' said Mr Tapper. 'He keeps himself to himself, does Mr Wooh. He may come and join us for supper, and he may not. As we're opening the circus tomorrow night, maybe he'll turn up tonight. I'm a bit scared of him, to tell you the truth.'

'But he's not a *real* wizard, is he?' asked Tinker.

'Well, when I talk to Mr Wooh I feel as if he is,' said Mr Tapper. 'There isn't a thing he doesn't know about figures, there isn't a thing he can't do with them. Ask him to multiply any number by any other number, running into dozens of figures, and he'll tell you in a second. He shouldn't be in a circus. He should be an inventor of some

90

sort – an inventor whose invention needs pages and pages of figures. He'd be happy then.'

'He sounds a bit like my father,' said Tinker. '*He's* an inventor, you know, and sometimes when I creep into his study I see papers FULL of millions of tiny figures and plans and diagrams with tiny figures all over them too.'

'Very interesting,' said Grandad. 'Your father and Mr Wooh ought to meet. They would probably talk figures all day long! My word – what's that you're handing round, young lady?'

'Some of the food *we* brought,' said Anne. 'Have a sausage or two, Mr Tapper – and a roll – and a tomato.'

'Well, thanks,' said Mr Tapper, pleased. 'Very kind of you. Nice to have met you all. You might be able to teach Jeremy a few manners!'

'Grandad – here's Mr Wooh!' said Jeremy, suddenly, and got up. Everyone turned round. *So this* was Mr Wooh, the Wonder Magician. Well, he certainly looked the part.

He stood there, with a half-smile on his face, tall, commanding and handsome. His hair was thick and black as soot, his eyes gleamed in the firelight, half hidden by great eyebrows, and he wore a thin, pointed beard. He had a curiously deep voice, and spoke with a foreign accent.

'So we have visitors this night?' he said, and showed a row of gleaming white teeth in a quick smile. 'May I join you?'

'Oh do, Mr Wooh,' said Anne, delighted to have the

91

chance of talking to a Wonder Magician. 'We've brought plenty of food. Do you like cold sausage – and tomato – and a roll?'

'Most deelicious!' said the magician, and sat down cross-legged to join the group.

'We were disappointed not to see you at the rehearsal,' said Dick. 'I'd have liked to hear you doing all kinds of wizard sums in your head, as quick as lightning!'

'My father can do that too,' said Tinker proudly. 'He's a wizard at figures as well. He's an inventor.'

'Ha! An inventor? And what does he invent?' asked Mr Wooh, eating his roll.

That was enough to set Tinker describing at once how wonderful his father was. 'He can invent *any*thing he's asked for,' said the boy, proudly. 'He invented a wonderful thing for keeping aeroplanes dead straight in the right direction – better than any idea before. He invented the sko-wheel, if you know what that is – and the electric trosymon, if you've ever heard of that. I don't suppose you have, though. They're too . . .'

'Wait, boy!' said Mr Wooh, sounding most interested. 'These things I have heard of, yes. I do not know them, but I have certainly heard of them. Your father must be a very, very clever man, with a most unusual brain.'

Tinker swelled with pride. 'Something got into the papers about his inventions a little while ago,' he said, 'and reporters came down to see Dad, and his name was in the papers – but Dad was awfully cross about it. You see,

he's in the middle of the biggest idea he's ever thought of and it messed up his work to have people coming to interview him – some of them even peered through the window, and went to see his wonderful tower, with its . . .'

'Tower? He has a tower?' said Mr Wooh, full of surprise. Before Tinker could answer, he received a hard poke from Julian's finger. He turned crossly, to see Julian

frowning fiercely at him. So was George. He went suddenly red in the face. Of course – he had been told never to
talk about his father's work. It was secret work, very
secret.

He pretended to choke over a piece of meat, hoping that
Julian would take the chance of changing the subject – and
Julian did, of course!

'Mr Wooh, could you do a bit of magic reckoning with
figures?' he asked. 'I've heard that you can give the
answers to any sum as quick as lightning.'

'That is true,' said Mr Wooh. 'There is nothing that I
cannot do with figures. Ask me anything you like, and I
will give you the answer at once!'

'Well, Mr Wooh, answer this then,' cried Tinker.
'Multiply sixty-three thousand, three hundred and forty-
two by eighty thousand, nine hundred and fifty-three! Ha
– you can't do that in a hurry!'

'The answer is, in figures, 5127724926,' said Mr Wooh
at once, with a slight bow. 'That is an easy question, my
boy.'

'Crumbs!' said Tinker, astounded. He turned to Julian.
'Is that right, Ju?'

Julian worked out the sum on paper. 'Yes. Absolutely
correct. Whew!' he said. 'You said that as quick as
lightning!'

'Let *me* give him a sum to do!' cried George. 'What do
you get if you multiply 602491 by 352, Mr Magician?'

'I get the figures 2–1–2–0–7–6–8–3–2,' said Mr Wooh,

immediately. And once more Julian worked out the sum on paper. He raised his head and grinned. 'Yes – correct. How do you do it so quickly?'

'Magic – just a little elementary magic!' answered Mr Wooh. 'Try it sometime yourself. I am sure that this boy's father would be as quick as I am!' He looked at Tinker. 'I should much like to meet your clever father, my boy,' he said in his deep voice. 'We would have much, so much to talk about. I have heard about his wonderful tower. A monument to his genius! Ah, you see, even we foreigners know of your father's great work. Surely he is afraid of having his secrets stolen?'

'Oh, I don't think so,' said Tinker. 'The tower is a pretty good hiding place, and . . .' He stopped suddenly, and went red again as he received an even harder kick from Julian. How *could* he be so stupid as to give away the fact that his father's secret plans and models were hidden in the tower!

Julian thought it was time to take Tinker firmly away from Mr Wooh and give him a good lecture on keeping his mouth shut. He looked at his watch, and pretended to be horrified at the time. 'Look. Do you know what the time is? Jenny will be ringing up the police if we don't get back straight away. Come on, Tinker, and you others, we *must* go. Thanks a lot, Grandad, for letting us share your supper.'

'But we haven't yet finished!' said Grandad. 'You haven't had enough to eat.'

95

FIVE ARE TOGETHER AGAIN

'We really couldn't eat any more,' said Dick, following Julian's determined lead. 'See you tomorrow, Grandad. Good night, Grandma. Thanks very much indeed.'

'We've still got bananas and apples to eat,' said Tinker, feeling obstinate.

'Oh, we brought those for Charlie the Chimp,' said Dick, not quite truthfully. He could have boxed Tinker's ears! Silly little idiot, couldn't he realise that Julian wanted to get him away from this cunning Mr Wooh? Wait till he got Tinker by himself!

Tinker found himself hustled on all sides, and felt a bit scared. Julian sounded rather fierce, he thought. Old Grandad was most astonished at the sudden departure of his guests – but Charlie the Chimp didn't mind! The guests had left behind a generous supply of fruit!

Over the fence they all went, with Julian hustling Tinker in front of him. Once over the fence and out of Mr Wooh's hearing, Julian and George rounded on the boy angrily.

'Are you mad, Tinker?' demanded Julian. 'Didn't you guess that that man was trying to pump you about your father's hush-hush job?'

'He wasn't,' said Tinker, almost in tears. 'You're just exaggerating!'

'Well, I hope *I* never try to give away *my* father's secret work!' said George, in a tone of such disgust that Tinker could have howled.

'I don't like him and I don't trust him,' said Julian,

sounding suddenly very grown up. 'But there you sat lapping up everything he said, ready to pour out all he wanted to know. I'm ashamed of you. You'd get a jolly good thrashing if your father had heard you. I only hope you haven't already said too much. You know how angry your father was when a report of his latest ideas got into the papers, and swarms of people came prying round the house . . .'

Tinker could stand it no longer. He gave a forlorn howl that made Mischief jump, and fled up the garden to the house, the little monkey running swiftly behind him. He wanted to comfort Tinker. What was the matter? Poor little Mischief felt bewildered, and tried his best to catch up with the sobbing Tinker. He caught him up at last, leapt to the boy's shoulder and put his little furry arms round Tinker's neck, making a funny comforting noise.

'Oh Mischief,' said Tinker. 'I'm glad *you're* still my friend. The others won't be now, I know. Aren't I an *idiot*, Mischief? But I was only being proud of my father, I was, really!'

Mischief clung to Tinker, puzzled and upset. Tinker stopped outside the tall tower. There was a light at the top. His father must still be working there. A faint humming noise came to his ears. He wondered if it was those strange, spindly tentacles right at the very top of the tower that made the noise.

Suddenly the light at the top of the tower went out.

Dad must have finished his work for tonight, thought Tinker. He'll be coming to the house. I'd better go. He might wonder why I'm all upset. Gosh, I never heard Julian be so angry before. He sounded as if he absolutely *despised* me!

He crept up the path that led to the house, and in at the garden door. Better not go and see Jenny. She might worm everything out of him, and be as disgusted with him as Julian was. She would wonder why he wasn't camping out with them! He'd go upstairs and sleep in his own bed tonight!

'Come on, Mischief,' he said, in a mournful voice. 'We'll go to bed, and you can cuddle down with me.

You'd never be mean to me, would you? You'd always be my friend.'

Mischief jabbered away, and the funny little monkey voice comforted Tinker all the time he undressed. He flung himself into bed, and Mischief lay at the bottom, on his feet. 'I shall never be able to get to sleep tonight,' said Tinker, still miserable. 'Never!'

But he fell asleep at once – which was a great pity, really. He might have shared in quite a bit of excitement, if he hadn't slept so soundly! Poor Tinker!

CHAPTER ELEVEN

In the dark of the night

JULIAN AND the others made no attempt to follow Tinker. 'Let him go, the little idiot!' said Julian. 'Come into one of the tents and have a low pow-wow before we get undressed and go to sleep.'

'I'm sorry poor old Tinker isn't going to camp out with us, our first night in the field,' said Anne. 'I don't think he *meant* to give anything away.'

'That's no excuse, Anne,' said George. 'He can be really stupid at times, and he's got to learn not to be. Let's go to our tent. I feel quite tired. Come along, Timmy!'

She yawned and Dick yawned too. Then Julian found himself yawning. 'Awfully catching, this yawning business!' he said. 'Well, it's turned out to be a lovely night as regards weather – warm and dry – and there's a nice little half-moon to look at. Good night, girls, sleep tight! And don't scream if a spider wakes you, because I warn you, I am NOT going to get up to deal with a harmless spider!'

'You wait till one runs all over *your* face!' said Anne, 'and starts making a web from your nose to your chin and catches flies in it!'

'Don't, Anne,' said George. 'I'm not a bit scared of

spiders, but that's a horrible idea of yours! Timmy, please watch out for spiders, and give me warning of them!'

Everyone laughed. 'Well, good night, girls,' said Dick. 'Pity about young Tinker. Still, he's got to learn a few things, and keeping his mouth shut is one of them.'

They were all quite tired, and it wasn't long before everyone's torch was out, and peace and quiet descended on the little camp. Much farther up the field the circus was also peaceful and quiet, though there were still lights here and there in the tents. Someone belonging to the circus band was strumming a banjo, but not loudly, and the sound was pleasant to hear – strum-a-strum – strum-a-strum – strummmm . . .

A few clouds blew up and slid across the moon. One by one the lights went out in the circus tents. The wind blew softly through the trees, and an owl hooted.

Anne was still awake. She lay listening to the wind, and to the owl's 'Too-whoo-too-whit', and then she, too, fell asleep. Nobody heard someone stirring in the circus camp. Nobody saw a shadowy figure creep out when the moon was safely behind a cloud. It was late, very late, and the two camps were lost in dreams.

Timmy was fast asleep too – but in his sleep he heard a faint sound, and at once he was awake. He didn't move, except for his ears which switched themselves to listen. He gave a little growl, but not enough to wake George. So long as the person who was moving about in the circus camp did not come near to George's tent, or the boys' tent,

FIVE ARE TOGETHER AGAIN

Timmy did not mean to bark. He heard a tiny grunt and recognised it at once. Charlie the Chimp! Well, that was all right! Timmy fell asleep again.

Tinker, too, was fast asleep in his bed up at the house, Mischief at his feet. He had thought he would be too miserable to sleep, but found himself half-dreaming in no time. He didn't hear a small noise outside, a very small noise indeed – a little scrape, as if someone's foot had caught against a stone. Then there came other very small noises – and a whisper of a voice – and more noises again.

Nobody heard anything at all until Jenny woke up thirsty, and stretched out her hand to get a glass of water from her bed table. She didn't switch her light on, and was about to lie down again when her quick ears caught a little sound.

She sat up. That can't be the children, she thought. They're camping down in the field. Oh my goodness me, I hope it's not a burglar – or someone trying to steal the Professor's secrets. He's got papers all over the place. Thank goodness he keeps most of them in that tower of his!

She listened, and then lay down again. But soon she heard another little noise, and sat up, scared. It sounds as if it comes from the tower, she thought, and got out of bed. No – there was no light in the tower – no light anywhere, that she could see. The moon was behind a cloud. She'd just wait till it slid out and lit up the courtyard below, and the tower. There! That was another little noise. Could it be

the wind? No, it couldn't. And now, what was *that*? It sounded just like someone whispering down there in the courtyard. Jenny felt really frightened, and began to shake. She must go and wake the Professor! Suppose it was someone after his precious papers? Or his wonderful new invention!

The moon swung out from behind the cloud and Jenny peered cautiously out of the window again. She gave a loud scream, and staggered back into her room, still screaming. 'There's a man! Help! Help! He's climbing up the wall of the tower! Professor! PROFESSOR HAYLING! Come quickly! Thieves, robbers, help, help! Get the police!'

There came a long slithering sound, and before Jenny dared to look out again, the moon had gone behind another cloud, and she could not see a thing in the sudden darkness. There was a deep silence after the slithering noise, and Jenny couldn't bear it. She rushed out of her bedroom, yelling at the top of her voice. 'THIEVES! ROBBERS! COME QUICKLY!'

The Professor woke with a jump, threw off his bedclothes and rushed out into the passage, almost colliding with Jenny. He clutched at her, thinking she was the thief, and she screamed again, sure that one of the intruders had got hold of her. They struggled together, and then the Professor realised that he wasn't holding a thief, he was holding poor, plump Jenny!

'JENNY! What on earth are you doing, waking up the

whole household!' said the Professor, switching on the passage light. 'Have you had a bad dream – a nightmare?'

'No, no,' panted Jenny, out of breath with her struggle. 'There's robbers about. I saw one climbing up the tower wall – and there must have been others below. I heard them whispering. Oh, I'm scared! What shall we do? Can you telephone for the police?'

'Well,' said the Professor, doubtfully. 'Are you quite sure, Jenny, that you didn't have a nightmare? I mean – if there really *are* robbers, I'll certainly telephone – but it's rather a long way for the police to come out here, and . . .'

'Oh – then won't you just take a torch and look round the place?' begged Jenny. 'You know there's your precious papers in that tower. And isn't there that new invention of yours? Oh yes, I know I'm not supposed to know anything about it, but I do dust your rooms thoroughly, you know, and I see quite a lot, though I keep my mouth shut, and . . .'

'Yes, yes, Jenny, I know,' said poor Professor Hayling, trying to stop Jenny's stream of talk. 'But honestly, everything seems quiet now. I've looked out into the courtyard. There's no one there. And you know as well as I do that nobody can get into my tower. It has three different keys – one to unlock the bottom door – one for the middle door, halfway up – and one for the top door. Jenny, be sensible. Nobody could have used my three keys. Look, there they are on my dressing-table.'

Jenny began to calm down, but she still wasn't satisfied. 'I *did* hear whispering, and I *did* see someone halfway up the wall of the tower. Please do come down with me, and let's look around. I daren't go on my own. But I shan't sleep again tonight till I know nobody's forced the tower door, or taken a ladder to go up the tower.'

'All right, Jenny,' said the Professor, with a sigh. 'Put on your dressing gown, and I'll put mine on too – we'll try the doors, and we'll look for a ladder – though, mind you, it would have to be an absolutely colossal one to reach the top of that tower. Nobody could possibly bring one that size and length into our small courtyard! All right, all right – we'll go.'

And so, a few minutes later, Jenny and the Professor were down in the courtyard. There was no sign of any ladder at all – no sign of anyone climbing up the wall – and the downstairs tower door was safely locked! 'You unlock the door, and go up to the top room and see if that door's locked too,' begged Jenny.

'I think you're being rather silly now, Jenny,' said the Professor impatiently. 'Here, take the keys yourself. This one's locked, of course – and if the middle door is still locked, you'll know nobody could have got into my top room. Hurry, Jenny.'

So Jenny, still trembling, slid a key into the bottom lock, opened the door, and began to climb the spiral stair that led upwards. Halfway was another door, also safely locked. She unlocked this too. She began to feel rather silly. Nobody could have gone through locked doors. And there now – the top one was well and truly locked also! She gave a sigh of relief and ran down the spiral stairway, locking the middle door, and then the bottom one. She gave the keys to the Professor, who by now was feeling rather chilly!

'All locked,' said Jenny. 'But I'm still sure someone was about. I could have sworn I saw someone up that tower wall, and heard somebody else whispering below.'

'I expect you were so scared that you imagined things, Jenny,' said the Professor, yawning. 'I think you'll agree with me that the wall is far too steep for anyone to climb – and I'm pretty certain I'd have heard it if a ladder had been dragged about the courtyard!'

'Well, I'm sure I'm very sorry,' said poor Jenny. 'It's a good thing we didn't wake Tinker – though I'm surprised Mischief didn't hear something and come running down the stairs.'

'But Mischief is surely with Tinker, camping out in the field!' said the Professor in surprise.

'No – Tinker and Mischief are back. I found them asleep in bed – but not the others!' said Jenny. 'Maybe Tinker had quarrelled with them. Funny that Mischief didn't come running out to see what was up – he must have heard us!'

'Mischief is clever – but not clever enough to open

FIVE ARE TOGETHER AGAIN

Tinker's bedroom door,' said the Professor, yawning again. 'Good night, Jenny. Don't worry. You'll feel all right in the morning, and that will be that!'

The Professor went sleepily to his room. He looked out of the window down into the courtyard and then across at the tower, and smiled. Dear Jenny! She did rather let her imagination run away with her! As if anyone in the world could get up into that tower room without a ladder! And HOW could a long, long ladder be brought into that small courtyard without either being seen or heard? The Professor yawned once more and climbed into bed.

But someone *had* been in the tower room! Someone very clever, someone very light-fingered! What a shock for poor Professor Hayling next morning when he crossed the courtyard, unlocked the bottom door of the tower – walked up the spiral stairway – unlocked the middle door, and went on up the stairway again – and finally unlocked the top door and opened it wide.

He stood and stared in horror. The place was upside down! All his papers were scattered everywhere. He crouched down at once to see if any were missing. Yes – quite a lot! But they seemed to have been taken quite haphazardly – a few pages from this notebook – a few pages from that – some letters he had written and left on his desk to post – and good gracious, the ink was spilt all over the place – and the little clock was gone from the mantelpiece. So Jenny was right – a thief *had* been about last night. A thief that could apparently get through three locked doors – or else could climb up a long, long ladder that he had put outside without being seen – and taken away again!

I'll have to ring the police, he thought. But I must say it's a mystery! I wonder if Tinker heard anything in the night? No, he couldn't have, or he would have run to fetch me. It's a mystery – a real puzzle of a MYSTERY!

CHAPTER TWELVE

A shock for Tinker

TINKER WAS horrified when Jenny told him the next morning what had happened. 'Your father's in a rare old state,' she said. 'He came down early this morning because he wanted to finish some work up in the tower – and as soon as he unlocked the top door into the tower room, he saw the whole room upside down and some of his precious papers gone, and . . .'

'JENNY! How awful!' said Tinker. 'Dad kept his most precious papers there – with all the figures for that new electric thing of his. It's a wonderful thing, too marvellous for words, Jenny, it's for . . .'

'Now don't you give away any of your father's plans, not even to *me*, said Jenny. 'You've been told that before. Maybe you've been talking too much already, and somebody's ears took it all in!'

Tinker suddenly felt sick. *Was* it because of something he had been silly enough to say in public? In the bus, perhaps? Or in the circus field? What would the others say – especially Julian – when they heard that someone had come in the night and stolen precious papers containing figures and diagrams for some of his father's inventions? Julian would be sure to say that it was *his* fault for not

110

keeping his mouth shut! Oh dear – would *this* be in the papers – and would hordes of people come visiting the place again, staring and whispering and exclaiming in awe at his father's curious tower with its waving tentacles?

He dressed quickly and ran downstairs. Jenny had told him that she was sure she had heard whispering down in the courtyard the night before, and had seen someone climbing up the tower. 'Your father says nobody could have brought a long ladder into that courtyard,' she said. 'Not without us seeing it, anyway, or hearing some kind of noise when it was dragged in. But it might have been a sliding ladder, mightn't it? That would be a smallish thing, with ropes to pull out the sliding part.'

FIVE ARE TOGETHER AGAIN

'Yes. Like the window cleaner uses,' said Tinker. '*It* couldn't have been the window cleaner, could it?'

'No. He's a really decent fellow,' said Jenny. 'I've known him for twenty years. So put *that* out of your head. But the ladder could certainly have been the sort that window cleaners use. We'll go out into the courtyard as soon as I've finished washing-up, and see if we can find the marks where the ladder was dragged over the courtyard. Though I must say I didn't hear any *dragging* noises. I heard whispering – and a kind of slithery noise – but that's all.'

'The slithery noise *might* have been made by the ladder when it was dragged along!' said Tinker. 'Hey – look at old Mischief. He's listening as if he understood every word. Mischief, why didn't you wake me up last night when all this was going on? You usually wake if anything unusual happens, or you hear a strange noise.'

Mischief leapt into Tinker's arms and cuddled there. He didn't like it when Tinker was upset about anything; he knew by the boy's voice that he was worried. He made small comforting noises, and rubbed his monkey nose against the boy's chin.

'You'd better go to your father,' said Jenny. 'You might be able to comfort him a little. He's very upset indeed. He's up in the tower room, trying to sort out his papers. My word, they were left in a state – scattered all over the room!'

Tinker stood up to go, and was astonished to find that

112

he was shaky at the knees. Would his father ask him if he had been talking about the work he was doing? Oh dear – he had even boasted about it just the day before, and talked about his father's sko-wheel, and the wonderful new machine, the electric trosymon! Tinker's knees became shakier than ever.

But, fortunately, his father was far too upset about his muddled room and missing papers to worry about anything Tinker had said or done. He was up in the tower room, trying to discover which of his papers were missing.

'Ah, Tinker,' he said, when the boy came into the tower room. 'Just give me a hand, will you? The thief who came last night must have knocked the whole bunch of papers off the table, down on the floor – and fortunately he seems not to have seen some that went under the table. So I doubt very much if the papers he *did* take away with him will be of any use. He'd need to be quite a scientist to understand them, without having the ones he left behind.'

'Will he come back for the others, then?' asked Tinker.

'Probably,' said his father. 'But I shall hide them somewhere. Can you think of a good hiding place, Tinker?'

'Dad – don't *you* hide them,' begged Tinker. 'Not unless you tell *me* where they are! You know how you forget things! You might forget where you'd put this bunch of papers, and then you wouldn't be able to go on with your inventions. Have you copies of the stolen sheets of figures and diagrams?'

'No. But they're all in my head as well as on paper,' said his father. 'It will take me a bit of time to work them all out again, but it can be done. It's a nuisance – especially as I'm working to a date. Now run along, Tinker, please. I've work to do.'

Tinker went down the spiral staircase of the tower. He'd have to make sure that his father *did* hide away those papers very carefully indeed – in some really good place. Oh dear – I hope he won't do what he did with the last lot of papers he wanted to hide, he thought. He stuffed them up the chimney – and they nearly went up in flames because Jenny thought she'd light the fire the next night, it was unexpectedly so cold. Good thing they fell down when she laid the fire and she rescued them before they got burnt! Why are brainy people like Dad so silly about ordinary things! I BET he'll either forget where he puts them – or go and hide them in some easy place where anyone could find them!

He went to talk to Jenny. 'Jenny – Dad says that the thief only took *some* of his papers – and that he can't make much use of the ones he took, unless he has the whole lot. And Dad says he thinks that when the thief finds this out, he'll try to steal the rest of the papers.'

'Well, let him try!' said Jenny. '*I* could hide them in a place where no thief would find them – if your Dad would let *me* have them. I shan't tell you where!'

'*I'm* afraid he might hide them up a chimney again, or some silly place like that,' said Tinker, looking so worried that Jenny felt really worried too! 'They've got to be hidden somewhere NOBODY would think of looking. And if Dad finds a place like that he'll promptly forget all about it, and never be able to find them again! But a thief might find them – he'd know ALL the places to look in.'

'Let's go up to the tower room and clear up the mess that the spilt ink made, and see if your father has taken his precious papers and hidden them somewhere there,' said Jenny. 'It would be just like him to hide them in the very room that the thief went to last night! Up the ladder, in at the window – left wide open, I've no doubt – snatched up every paper he could see, the rogue, and then raced down the ladder again!'

'Come on up to the tower, then,' said Tinker. 'I only hope Dad isn't there!'

'He's just crossing the courtyard, look,' said Jenny, leaning out of the window. 'See, there he is – carrying something under his arm.'

'His morning newspapers,' said Tinker. 'It looks as if he's going to have a jolly good read, doesn't it? Oh dear, I do hope all this won't be printed in the newspapers – it would bring hordes of people down here again. Do you remember how awful it was last time, Jenny – people even walked over the flower-beds!'

'Hoo – some people like to poke their noses into everything!' said Jenny. 'I don't mind telling you that I emptied my dirty washing water out of the window on to a few of them – quite by mistake, of course – how was *I* to know they were out there, staring up and down?'

Tinker gave a shout of laughter. 'I wish I'd seen that!' he said. 'Oh Jenny – if people come poking their noses into Dad's business again, DO let's empty water on their silly heads! Come on, Jenny – let's go up to the tower room now Dad's out of the way. Quick!'

They were soon out in the courtyard and, as they crossed it, Jenny stopped and looked hard at the ground.

'What are you looking for?' asked Tinker.

'Just to see if there are any marks that might have been made by someone dragging a ladder across,' said Jenny. 'I heard a funny slithering sound, you know but it didn't *sound* like a ladder being dragged across.'

The two of them looked all over the courtyard, but could see no marks there that could possibly have been made by a ladder.

'Funny,' said Jenny. 'It worries me, that slithery sound.' She looked up at the tall, steep wall of the tower. It was made of flint-stones of all shapes and sizes, the kind found in the countryside round about Kirrin and Big Hollow.

'Well, I suppose a *cat* might climb up,' said Jenny, doubtfully. 'But not a *man*. He'd slip sooner or later. It would be far too dangerous. I doubt if even a cat would get far.'

'And yet you say you thought you saw someone up the tower wall!' said Tinker. 'Go on, Jenny – it must have been the shadow of a passing cloud that you saw! Look up this

116

wall – now can you imagine ANYONE climbing up it at night, when it was dark?'

Jenny stared up. 'No – you're right. Only a madman would even try. Well, my eyes must have played me up, then, when I looked out last night – but I really *did* think I saw a dark shadow climbing up the tower wall. Still, it's easy to be mistaken at night. And I don't believe there was a ladder, either! There *would* be marks on the paving-stones of the courtyard if there had been a ladder. Oh well – let's hurry on up to the tower room before your Dad decides to go back to it again!'

They went up the spiral stairway. All the doors were unlocked, as it was plain that the Professor was going to come back again after he had read his papers.

'All the same – he shouldn't leave the doors unlocked, even for a minute!' said Jenny. 'Well, here we are – just look at the ink splashes everywhere – and that dear little clock that kept such good time is gone. Now what would the thief want with a clock, I'd like to know?'

'It would be small and neat enough to pop into his pocket,' said Tinker. 'If he was dishonest enough to steal Dad's papers, he would certainly not say no to a nice little clock like that! He's probably taken other things too!'

They went right into the room, and Jenny at once gave a loud exclamation. 'LOOK! Aren't those some of the papers your father was working on – on the table there? All covered with tiny figures?'

A SHOCK FOR TINKER

Tinker looked closely at them. 'Yes – they're his very latest papers. He showed me them the other day. I remember this diagram. Jenny – how COULD he leave them on the table with the door unlocked this morning – when only last night the thief was here! How could he? He *said* he was going to hide them away so carefully, because, if the thief found them, he could use them with the other papers that were stolen – but as long as the thief only had half of them, they wouldn't be much use – and now he's forgotten all about hiding them, after all!'

'Look now, Tinker – let's hide them away ourselves,' said Jenny, 'and not tell him where they are. These thieves will have another try for them, no doubt about that. Let's think of some place where they'd be absolutely safe.'

'*I* know!' said Tinker. 'We could hide them on Kirrin Island! Somewhere in the old ruined castle! NOBODY would guess they were there.'

'Now that's a *fine* idea!' said Jenny. 'I'd be glad to think they were out of the house.' She gathered up the papers quickly. 'Here you are. You'd better tell Julian and the others, and go across to the island with them as soon as you can. My, what a relief to think they'll be well away from here. I'll be able to sleep soundly in my bed at nights then!'

Tinker stuffed the precious papers under his jersey, and he and Jenny ran at top speed down the spiral stairway. They saw the Professor not far off, and he turned and hailed them. 'Tinker! Jenny! I know what you're going to ask me! You want to know where I've hidden those papers of mine. Come here and I'll whisper!'

Not knowing quite what to say, the two went rather guiltily over to Tinker's father. He whispered loudly, 'I've wrapped them up, and put them under the coal at the back of the coal-cellar – right at the *very* back!'

'And a fine mess you've made of your trousers,' said Jenny, disgusted. 'And good gracious – you must have sat down in the coal yourself! You look a right mess. Come along and let me brush you down. Not indoors, though, or the place will be thick with coal-dust!'

'Don't you think it was a good hiding place, Jenny?' asked the Professor. 'Ha – you thought I'd forget to hide them, didn't you?'

He went off, looking very pleased with himself. Jenny chuckled in delight. 'Dear old Professor! He's hidden all his *newspapers* there, but not a single one of his own precious papers. And now whatever shall we tell him when he wants the morning papers? Tinker, you cycle out to the paper shop and get another lot. My goodness – what it is to have a brainy man in the house! Whatever will he do next?'

CHAPTER THIRTEEN

Quite a lot of plans!

AFTER TINKER had fetched a new supply of morning papers, he decided to go down to the camp in the field and tell the others all that had happened that morning. He still felt angry about being ticked off by Julian the night before – but he simply couldn't wait to tell the others about the robbery – and about the grand idea he, Tinker, had of hiding the rest of his father's papers on Kirrin Island.

So off he went, with Mischief happily on his shoulder, holding tightly to his hair. The others were all there in the field. They had just come back from a shopping expedition, and Tinker's eyes gleamed when he saw the various tinned meats and tinned fruits, fresh rolls, tomatoes and apples and bananas that had been brought back from the shops at Big Hollow.

Julian was glad to see that Tinker looked bright and cheerful. He was afraid that the boy might have sulked, and that would have spoilt things for the others.

'Hi!' said Tinker. 'I've got news!' And he proceeded to tell the others all about the happenings of the night before, ending up with his father solemnly going off to hide his morning newspapers under the coal at the back of the

121

coal-cellar, under the impression that he was hiding the rest of his precious papers.

'But why on earth didn't you tell him he had left his valuable papers behind and hidden his newspapers?' asked George.

'Because, if he knew that, he'd go and hide the *precious* papers somewhere, and forget where he'd put them – and they might be lost for ever!' said Tinker.

'Well, what are *you* going to do with them?' asked Dick.

'I've had rather a brainwave,' said Tinker, as modestly as he could. 'Er – I thought that *we'd* hide them away ourselves, where nobody could *possibly* find them.'

'And where is this wonderful hiding place?' asked Dick.

QUITE A LOT OF PLANS!

'On Kirrin Island!' said Tinker, triumphantly. 'Who'd think of looking *there*? And as we shall *all* know the hiding place, we can't possibly forget it. The papers will be absolutely safe. Dad can get on with the rest of his ideas without worrying about anything?'

'Have you told him all this?' asked Julian.

'Well, no,' said Tinker. 'Jenny thought we'd better just keep it to ourselves. She's pretty certain the thieves will try their hand at breaking in to get the rest of the papers, though.'

'Ha! Well, I vote we scribble some papers ourselves,' said Dick. 'Complete with wonderful diagrams, and all kinds of peculiar figurings and numberings. I feel I could do that very well! And we'd leave them up in the tower room for the thieves to take – they'd think they were the ones they'd missed!'

Everyone chuckled. 'Idiot!' said Julian. 'Still – it's not a bad idea to leave something behind for the thieves that isn't worth a moment's look – and hide the genuine figures where they'd never dream of finding them – on Kirrin Island!'

'When shall we go?' asked George. 'It's ages since I've visited my island – and will you believe it, last time I rowed over *trippers* had been there and left their beastly mess everywhere! Paper bags, broken glass, lettuce leaves, orange peel, ugh!'

'Why DO people do that?' asked Anne. 'They'd hate to have to sit in the midst of *other* people's mess – so why in the world can't they clear up their own?'

'Oh, they're probably just like that in their own homes,' said Dick. 'All mess and litter – and yet it takes so little time to clear up a picnic mess, and leave the place decent for the next comers.'

'What did you do with all the mess left on Kirrin Island?' asked Julian.

'I buried it deep in the sand at the back of one of the beaches,' said George. 'Where the tide can't turn it all up again. And with every dig of my spade I said "Blow you, you awful trippers without manners, blow you – and next time you go anywhere, may you find someone else's litter to make you feel sick. Blow you!"'

George looked and sounded so very fierce that everyone burst out laughing. Timmy sat there with his tongue lolling out, looking as if he were laughing too, and Mischief made a funny little noise rather like a giggle.

'Good old George. She always says straight out what she thinks!' said Julian.

They sat and talked over their plans for some time. 'Dick and Julian had better make the fake plans and figures,' said George. 'They'd be better at that kind of thing than anyone else. And Tinker can plant them somewhere in his father's tower room for the thief to take if he goes there again – and I bet he will. He found it easy enough last night!'

'And George could take Tinker's father's papers with the *correct* figures and plans over to Kirrin Island,' said Anne.

124

QUITE A LOT OF PLANS!

'Not till night time, though,' said Dick. 'If anyone were on the watch, and saw George rowing over there, they might guess she was taking something important to hide. They might be watching her father too. By the way – where *are* these papers? You did not leave them behind at home, did you, Tinker?'

'I didn't dare to,' said Tinker. 'I felt as if there might be eyes peeping at me, watching and hoping I'd go out and leave the papers behind. I've got them under my jersey, just here!' And he patted the top of his stomach.

'Oh – so *that*'s why you look as if you've had too much breakfast!' said George. 'Well – what shall our plans be?'

'We'd better make out the false papers straight away, with figures and diagrams,' said Julian. 'Just in case thieves come sooner than we think. Tinker, we'd better go into *your* house to do those. If we go to George's her father might spot us and wonder what on earth we were doing. We'd probably be sent off, anyway, because of the scarlet fever business.'

'Well, what about *my* father?' said Tinker. '*He* might spot us too. Anyway, he's not keen on my having anyone there this week, because he's so busy with his new invention. It's awfully good, and . . .'

'*Tinker* – don't start spilling beans again!' said Julian, warningly. 'I say it would be best to go to your house.'

'What about *me* going indoors and bringing out Dad's big drawing-board, and some of his paper, and his mapping pens and ink, and doing the diagrams and

125

things out here in the tent?' said Tinker. 'Honestly, I never know when Dad is going to come into my room. He'd wonder what on *earth* we were doing if he found us all there! We can have a good look at the papers I've got under my jersey, and do a whole lot in the same style – not the *same* figures, naturally – and we could do some diagrams too.'

'All right,' said Julian, giving way, as he saw that Tinker was genuinely afraid that his father might see them making the false papers. 'Go and get the drawing-board and come back with it, and anything else we'll need. You go with him, George.'

'Right,' said George, and she and Tinker went up Tinker's garden to the house. Tinker scouted round to see if his father was anywhere about, but couldn't see him. He found a large drawing-board, some big sheets of paper used by his father for working out his figures, and a book of odd but easy-to-copy diagrams. He also brought mapping pens, Indian ink and blotting-paper, and even remembered drawing-pins to pin the sheets of paper to the board. George carried half the things, and kept a sharp lookout for Tinker's father.

'It's all right. He's asleep somewhere – can't you hear that noise?' asked Tinker; and sure enough George could – a gentle snoring from some room not far off!

They went back down the garden and over the fence, handing everything to the others before they climbed over. 'Good!' said Julian. 'Now we can produce some beautiful

126

charts of figures that mean absolutely nothing at all – and diagrams that will look perfect and not mean a thing either!'

'Better come into the tent,' said George. 'If anyone wanders down from the circus camp, they might ask us what we're doing.'

So they all went into the boys' tent, which was the bigger one, Timmy too, and Mischief, who was delighted to be with the big dog. Julian soon set to work, though he found the space rather cramped. They were all watching him in admiration as he set out rows of beautiful, meaningless, figures when Timmy suddenly gave a deep growl, and all his hackles rose up on his neck.

Julian turned the drawing-board over at once, and sat on it. The canvas doorway of the tent was pulled aside and in poked the grinning face of Charlie the Chimp!

'Oh, it's *you*, Charlie!' said Julian. 'Well, well, well, and how are you today?'

The chimpanzee grinned even more widely, and held out his hand. Julian shook it solemnly, and the chimpanzee went carefully all round the tent, shaking hands with everyone.

'Sit down, Charlie,' said Dick. 'I suppose you've let yourself out of your cage as usual, and come to see what we've got for our dinner. Well, you'll be glad to hear we've got enough for you as well as ourselves.'

Charlie squashed himself between Timmy and Tinker, and with much interest watched Julian at work with his pen and ink. 'I bet that chimp could draw, if you gave him a piece of paper and a pencil,' said Anne.

So, to keep him quiet, he was given a pencil, and a notebook. He at once began to scribble in it very earnestly.

'Goodness – he's doing a whole lot of funny figures!' said Anne. 'He's trying to copy *you*, Ju!'

'If he's not careful, I'll hand the whole job over to him!' said Julian, with a chuckle. 'George, let's talk about your plans for tonight. I think, if you are going over to Kirrin Island to hide those papers, you must take Timmy with you.'

'Oh, I will!' said George. 'Not that there will be a single soul on the island, but I'd like old Tim just for company. I'll take the papers straight to the island, land, and hide them.'

'Where?' asked Julian.

'Oh, I'll decide that when I'm there,' said George. 'Somewhere cunning! I know my own little island from top to bottom. And there those papers will stay until all danger is past. We'll let Professor Hayling think he has hidden them somewhere himself, and forgotten where! It will be fun to row across to my island at night, with Timmy.'

'The thieves can make do with *my* figures and diagrams if they come to the tower room again,' said Julian. 'Don't they look professional?'

They certainly did! Everyone looked at the neat figures and carefully drawn diagrams with admiration.

QUITE A LOT OF PLANS!

Timmy suddenly sat up and gave a deep growl again. Charlie the Chimp patted him as if to say 'What's wrong, old boy?' but Timmy took no notice and went on growling. He suddenly shot out of the tent, and there was a shout from someone outside. 'Get off! Get down! GET DOWN!'

George swung back the tent opening. Mr Wooh was there, looking extremely frightened as Timmy growled menacingly round his ankles. Charlie the Chimp ran up to him on all fours and, angry because Timmy was snarling at his friend, showed his teeth suddenly at the big dog. George was terrified. 'Don't let them fight!' she cried, afraid that Timmy would get decidedly the worst of it. Charlie was jumping up and down in a most alarming way.

'Charleee!' said Mr Wooh in his deep voice. 'Charleee!'

And Charlie stopped jumping up and down and making horrible noises, and leapt straight on to Mr Wooh's back, putting his arms round his neck.

Mr Wooh bowed courteously to them all. 'I trust I have not disturbed you, my friends,' he said, with his strong accent. 'I'll now take a little walk with my friend Charleee. You come again to see our show, I hope. Yes? No?'

'Probably,' said Dick, noticing that the magician had taken a quick and interested look at Julian's figures and diagrams. Julian covered them up immediately, as if he didn't want the magician to see them. He had seen something in the man's eyes that puzzled him. Could Mr Wooh

129

possibly have had anything to do with the theft of the papers the night before? After all, he was a wizard at figures himself – he might be able to read the Professor's figures and diagrams and understand them perfectly. Well – he wouldn't gather much from the ones Julian was now doing – they were more or less nonsense made up by Julian himself to deceive anyone interested in the real ones.

'I interrupt you? Pardon me!' said Mr Wooh, and bowed himself politely away from the group in the tent. Charlie the Chimp followed him, hoping that Mischief would too, so that they could have a game. But Mischief didn't want to. He didn't like Mr Wooh.

'Well, I didn't realise that anyone from the circus would walk down the field so quietly, and be able to hear what we were saying inside the tent,' said Julian, worried. 'I didn't like the look in his eyes. Dick – you don't suppose he heard anything we were saying, do you?'

'Would it matter?' said Dick.

'It might,' said Julian. 'Do you think he heard what George said about going over to Kirrin Island with the other papers – the valuable ones that the thieves didn't see in the tower room last night? I wouldn't let George go if I thought he had heard. In fact, I think she'd better *not* go. She might run into danger.'

'Don't be silly, Ju,' said George. 'I *am* going. And Timmy will be with me.'

'You heard what I said, George. You are *not* to go!' said Julian. '*I'll* take the papers and hide them on the island. I'll get them when it's dark, fairly late. I'll cycle over to Kirrin and untie the boat you keep there, and row over to the island.'

'All right, Julian,' said George, astonishingly meekly. 'Shall we have a meal now? We've only to open the tins, and empty the tomatoes and lettuces out of the basket there. And the drinks are in that cool corner over there.'

'Right,' said Julian, glad that George had given way to him so easily. *He* would go across in George's boat and find a good hiding place. If danger was about, he reckoned he could deal with it better than George could.

Yes, Julian, you may be right. But don't be too sure about tonight!

CHAPTER FOURTEEN

Ladders – and a lot of fun!

THE CHILDREN stared after Mr Wooh and the chimpanzee. They saw Charlie pick up two empty buckets, one in each strong paw, and race off to the right with them.

'Where's he going?' said Anne, astonished at the rate he was running along.

'I bet he's going to get some water from the stream in those pails, and take them to whoever washes down the

horses,' said George. She was right! Charlie soon came back again, walking this time, holding a heavy pail of water in each hand!

'Well, I must say that chimpanzee is jolly useful!' said Dick. 'Look – there's Madelon who trains those beautiful horses that paraded round the ring last night – she's wearing old trousers this morning, she looks quite different. There – Charlie has set the pails of water down beside her. I bet that as soon as she wants any more water, he'll be off again to the stream!'

'I rather like old Charlie,' said Anne. 'I didn't at first – but now I do. I wish he didn't belong to Mr Wooh.'

Julian stood up, looking down at the paper on which he had so carefully written lines of small figures and drawn many peculiar diagrams. 'I somehow feel this isn't much good now,' he said. 'I think Mr Wooh must have guessed it was all a make-up as soon as he saw it. He gave himself away a bit, though – I saw him looking at the paper in a rather startled way, as if he'd seen something very like it very recently indeed!'

'So he had, the wretch, if he'd sent someone up to get my dad's papers out of the tower room!' said Tinker. 'Hey! What about having a look round the circus to see if we can spot a ladder anywhere – one tall enough to reach the tower room!'

'Good idea!' said Dick. 'Come on – we'll go now. Chuck that drawing-board and diagram paper over our fence, Ju. I hardly think it's worth your while to finish it.'

LADDERS – AND A LOT OF FUN!

The Five, with Tinker and Mischief, wandered down the field to where the circus was encamped. Dick spotted a ladder lying in the grass, and nudged Julian.

'Julian! See that? Would it reach the tower?' Julian walked over to it. It certainly was very, very long – but *would* it be long enough? No – he didn't think it would. Still – he might as well find out who owned it. At that moment up came the Boneless Man, walking perfectly. He grinned at the children – and then suddenly put all his double-joints to work, bent his knees into peculiar positions, twisted his head round so that he was looking over his own back, and then bent his double-jointed arms the wrong way, so that he looked very odd indeed!

'Don't! I don't like it!' said Anne. 'You look so peculiar and strange! Why are you called the *Boneless* Man? You aren't boneless – you just make yourself *look* as if you were, with all those funny double-joints of yours!'

The Boneless Man seemed suddenly to lose all his bones, and crumpled up on the grass in a funny heap. The children couldn't help laughing. He didn't look as if he had any bones at all then!

'Er – can you climb ladders if you're double-jointed?' asked Julian, suddenly.

'Of course!' said the Boneless Man. 'Run up them backwards, forwards, sideways – any way you like.'

'Is that *your* ladder, then?' asked Dick, nodding his head towards the ladder in the grass.

'Well – I use it, but so does everyone else!' said the

Boneless Man, turning his head the wrong way round, so that it seemed as if it was put on back to front. It was odd to speak to someone whose head did that – one minute they were talking to his face, the next to the back of his head!

'I *wish* you wouldn't do that,' said Anne. 'It makes me feel giddy.'

'Do you use that ladder to put the flag on the top of the circus tent?' asked Dick. 'It doesn't look long enough for that.'

'It isn't,' said the Boneless Man, turning his head the right way round, much to Anne's relief. 'There's a much longer one over there – it takes three men to carry it, it's so heavy – but the centre circus pole is very tall, as you see. One man couldn't *possibly* carry the long ladder.'

The children looked at one another. That ruled out the very long ladder too, then. If it needed three men to carry it, Jenny would certainly have heard a lot more noise last night!

'Are there any more ladders in the circus camp?'

'No – just the two. Why? Thinking of buying one?' said the Boneless Man. 'I must go. The Boss is beckoning to me.' Off he went, walking in a most peculiar fashion, using his double-joints for all he was worth!

'What about the acrobats?' said Julian. '*They* must be used to climbing and clambering everywhere. I wonder if any of *them* could have climbed the wall?'

'I don't think so,' said Tinker. 'I had a good look at it

136

this morning – and although there *is* a kind of creeper climbing up the wall, it stops halfway – and above that there's just the stone wall. Even an acrobat would have to have some help up the tower wall!'

'Could the *clowns* have found a way?' said George. 'No – I suppose they're not as good even as the acrobats at climbing. I don't believe the thief *could* have been anyone from the circus after all. Look – what's that on the ground over there – outside that tent?'

They all went over to see. It looked like a pile of dark-grey fur. George touched it with her toe. 'Oh – *I* know what it is – the donkey-skin!'

'Golly – so it is!' cried Tinker in delight, and picked it up – or tried to. It was much too heavy for him to hold up all of it.

In a trice Dick and George were inside that donkey-skin! Dick had the head, and found that he *could* see quite well where he was going, for the donkey neck had neat eye-holes in it – the head itself was stuffed with paper. George was the back legs, and kicked up her feet and made the donkey look extremely lively. The others roared with laughter.

Someone shouted loudly. 'Hey – you leave that donkey-skin alone!'

It was Jeremy. He came running up, looking furious. He had a stick in his hand, and hit out at the donkey's hind parts, giving poor George a good old whack, and making her yell.

LADDERS – AND A LOT OF FUN!

'Hey! Stop that, it hurt!'

Tinker looked furiously at Jeremy. 'How dare you do that?' he shouted. 'Dick and George are in the donkey-skin. Put down that stick!'

But Jeremy gave the donkey's hind legs another whack and George yelled again. Tinker gave a shout too, and flung himself on Jeremy, trying to get the stick out of his hand. The boy struggled, holding on to the stick, but Tinker gave him a straight blow on the chest, and down he went!

'Ha! I *said* I'd knock you down sometime, and I have!' yelled Tinker. 'Get up and fight. *I'll* teach you not to hit animals!'

'Now stop it, Tinker,' said Julian. 'Come out of the skin, you two idiots, before old Grandad comes up. He looks as if he's on his way now!'

Jeremy was up now, and danced round Tinker with doubled fists. Before either boy could exchange a blow, Grandad's great voice came to them.

'NOW THEN! STOP IT!'

Jeremy swung his fist at Tinker, who dodged, and then in his turn hit out at Jeremy, who ran back – straight into old Grandad, who at once clutched him.

By this time George and Dick were out of the donkey-skin, looking rather ashamed of themselves. Old Grandad grinned at them, still holding on to the furious Jeremy. 'Fight's off,' said Grandad to Tinker and Jeremy. 'If you want to go on, either of you, you can fight *me*, not each other.'

FIVE ARE TOGETHER AGAIN

However, neither of the boys wanted to take on old Grandad. He might be old, but he could still give some mighty slaps, as Jeremy very well knew. They stood staring at one another, looking rather sheepish.

'Go on – shake hands and be friends,' said Grandad. 'Quick, now, or I'll do a little fighting myself!'

Tinker held out his hand just as Jeremy held out his. They shook, grinning at one another. 'That's right!' said old Grandad. 'No harm done. No bones broken. You're quits now, so no more knocking each other about.'

'Right, Grandad,' said Jeremy, giving him a friendly punch. The old man turned to Dick and George. 'And if *you* want to borrow that donkey-skin, you're welcome,' said old Grandad. 'But it's manners to ask the owner's permission first.'

'Yes. Sorry,' said Dick, grinning. He wondered what Professor Hayling and Jenny would say if he and George did borrow it, and galloped into Hollow House at top speed. But no – he decided reluctantly that Jenny might be scared stiff and give notice, and that would never do. She wouldn't at all like being chased by an apparently mad donkey, nor would Professor Hayling.

Grandad went off, and Julian spoke to Jeremy, who wasn't quite sure whether to go or to stay. 'We saw old Charlie carrying pails of water for the horses,' he said. 'Isn't he strong!'

Jeremy grinned, glad to be friends again, and to be able to stay with the Five and Tinker. They wandered all round the field together, looking at the magnificent horses and at Dead-Shot Dick doing a little practising at shooting and then watched one small acrobat practising amazing jumps and somersaults.

Mischief the monkey came with them. He was absolutely at home with everyone in the circus now, man, woman or animal. He leapt on to the horses' backs, and they didn't mind! He pretended to help Charlie the Chimp to carry one of the pails of water – he ran off with Dead-Shot Dick's cap. He went into the chimp's cage and cuddled up in the straw with him, scrabbling about as if the cage belonged to him. He even went into Grandad's tent and came out with a small bottle of lemonade! He couldn't get the top off, and took it to Charlie, who was watching nearby! Charlie promptly forced it off with his strong front paws – and then, to Mischief's disgust, tipped up the bottle and drank the lot!

Mischief was very angry indeed. He ran to Charlie's cage, which was open, and sent the straw flying everywhere. Charlie sat outside his cage and enjoyed the fun, grinning happily.

'Come out, Mischief!' called Tinker. 'You're making a nuisance of yourself!'

'Let him be,' said one of the acrobats, who was standing nearby. 'Old Charlie enjoys a bit of temper – when it's someone else's! Look at him sitting grinning there.'

They watched for a few seconds more, to make sure that Mischief wasn't annoying the big chimpanzee, and then turned to watch Monty and Winks, the clowns, having an argument, which ended in Monty throwing water over Winks, and Winks emptying a basket of rubbish over Monty. What a pair!

When they turned to see if Mischief was still annoying Charlie, they saw that the little monkey had left the cage, and was tearing down the field to the fence. He leapt up, and over, and disappeared.

'He must think it's dinner time,' said Tinker, looking at his watch. 'And gosh, so it is. Come on everyone, Jenny will be in a fine old fury if we're really late – it's hot dinner today.'

Away they all went in a hurry. Hot dinner! Over the fence, then, and up the garden at top speed. They mustn't keep a hot dinner waiting – or Jenny either!

CHAPTER FIFTEEN

A happy day – and a shock for Julian

TINKER AND the Five were two minutes late for their dinner. Jenny was just taking it in, looking a little grim, as she had not been able to find the children anywhere. 'Ah – here you are at last!' she said. 'I looked down the garden but you were nowhere to be seen. It's a good thing you came in when you did – five minutes more and I'd have taken the dinner back again.'

'*Dear* Jenny, you know you wouldn't,' said Tinker, giving her a sudden squeeze that made her squeal. 'Oh, how good it smells! Mmmmm-mmmmm!'

'You and your mmmmms!' said Jenny, pushing Tinker away. 'And I've told you before, that I don't mind a gentle hug, but those *squeezes* of yours take all my breath away. *No*, Tinker, keep away from me – another squeeze like that and I'll feel like a lemon!'

Everyone laughed at that. Jenny did say the most amusing things. Anne felt sorry that she hadn't offered to stay and help her with the dinner. Oh dear – the time went so quickly, once they were all out together.

The talk at dinner time was very lively. So was Mischief the monkey! He took bits from everyone's plate and handed some of them down to Timmy, who was lying under the table as usual. Timmy appreciated these titbits very much!

'Well! *I* didn't see a single ladder in the circus camp that was tall enough to reach up to the tower room,' said George.

'No. If there was one, it was jolly well hidden,' said Dick. 'Pass the mustard, someone!'

'In front of you, idiot,' said Julian. 'You know I'm beginning to wonder if Mr Wooh had anything to do with the stealing of your father's papers, Tinker. I can't somehow see him climbing high ladders – he's so – so . . .'

'Polite and proper,' said Anne. 'Actually, I can't think of *any*one in the circus who would either *want* the papers, or is nasty enough to steal them. They're all so nice.'

'I still think Mr Wooh is the most *likely* one,' said Julian. 'He's interested in complicated figures and clever inventions. But all the same, I'm beginning to think I'm wrong. He could NOT have got up to the tower room as there is no ladder long enough – and I really doubt if he'd *dare* to take a ladder into the courtyard and risk putting it up to the tower. He might so easily be caught.'

'Right. We'll rule him out,' said Tinker. 'But if nobody went up the spiral stairway, because all doors were locked, and nobody used a ladder, I don't see HOW those papers disappeared.'

'Wind took them out of the window, perhaps?' suggested Anne. 'Would that be possible?'

'No. For two reasons,' said Julian. 'One is that the

window wasn't wide enough open for the wind to blow in with enough strength to blow papers *out*. And secondly, we'd have been sure to have found some of them down in the courtyard if they'd been blown out. But we didn't find a single one there.'

'Well – if nobody got through the three locked doors, and nobody got through the window, HOW did those papers get stolen?' demanded George. 'It would have been a miracle for those papers to have hopped away by themselves – and I don't believe in that kind of miracle!'

There was a long silence. What a mystery it was! 'I suppose Tinker's father couldn't *possibly* have gone walking in his sleep, and taken them, could he?' asked Anne.

'Well – I don't know if a sleep-walker can unlock doors with the right keys, and steal his own papers, leaving some on the floor, and then walk carefully down the spiral stairway still fast asleep, locking all the doors behind him, and then go to his own bedroom, get into bed, and then wake up in the morning without remembering a single moment of the whole thing!' said Julian.

'No. It can't be possible,' said Dick. 'Have you ever known your father to walk in his sleep, Tinker?'

Tinker considered. 'No, I can't say I have,' he said. 'He's a very light sleeper, usually. No. I don't believe Dad did all that in his sleep. It was somebody else.'

'It must have been some sort of miracle man, then,' said George. 'No *ordinary* person could do it. And whoever planned it wanted those papers very, very badly, or he would never have risked getting them against so many odds.'

'And if he wanted them so VERY badly, he'll certainly make an effort to get the ones he left behind under the table,' said Julian. 'Good thing we've got those! He will probably try to get up into the tower the same way as he did before – but goodness knows what it was!'

'Well – those papers will be safely out of his way, tonight!' said George. 'On my island!'

'Yes,' said Julian. 'I'll find a most unlikely hiding place – somewhere about the ruined castle, I think. By the way – I hope you haven't *still* got them under your jersey, Tinker. No – you don't look fat any more. What have you done with them?'

'George said I'd better give them to her to keep, in case they slipped out of my jersey,' said Tinker. 'You took them, didn't you, George?'

'Yes,' said George. 'Don't let's talk about it any more.'

'Why not? The thief's not here. He can't be listening to us!' said Tinker. 'I believe you're cross, George, because Julian won't let you take the papers yourself!'

'Oh, do shut up, Tinker,' said George. 'I shall be jolly cross with *you* in a minute, if you let Mischief upset your glass of lemonade again, all over my bread. Take him off the table! His manners are getting worse!'

'They aren't – but your temper is!' said Tinker and promptly received a kick under the table from Julian. He was about to kick back but thought better of it. Julian

could kick very much harder than he could! He decided to
take Mischief off the table in case George smacked him.
He put the little monkey under the table where Timmy was
sitting quietly. Mischief immediately cuddled up to him,
putting his little furry arms round the big dog's neck.
Timmy sniffed him all over, and then gave him two or
three licks. He was very fond of the naughty little monkey.

'What shall we do this afternoon?' asked Dick, when
they had all helped Jenny to clear away and wash up.
'What about a bathe in the sea? Is it warm enough?'

'Not really. But that doesn't matter, we always feel
warm when we come out of the water and run about
and then rub ourselves down,' said Anne. 'Jenny – do *you*
feel like a bathe?'

'Good gracious, no!' said Jenny, shivering at the
thought. 'I'm a cold mortal, I am. The thought of going
into that cold sea makes me shudder. If you want your
towels, they are all in the airing cupboard. And don't you
be late for tea, if you want any, because I've a lot of
ironing to do afterwards.'

'Right, Jenny,' said Tinker, about to give her one of his
'squeezes' but thinking better of it when he saw her
warning look. 'Julian, may I come with you to Kirrin
Island tonight? I'd like a bit of fun.'

'You may not,' said Julian. 'Anyway, there won't be any
fun.'

'There might be if Mr Wooh did hear George say she
was taking those papers over,' said Tinker. 'He'd be

waiting on the island – and you might be glad to have me with you!'

'I should *not* be glad to have you with me,' said Julian. 'You'd just be in the way. It would be much easier to look after myself than to see what *you* were up to all the time. I am going by myself. Please don't scowl at me like that, George.'

He got up from the table and went to look out of the window. 'Wind's died down a bit,' he said. 'I think I'll have a bathe in an hour's time. If any of you others want to come, we'll go down together.'

They all went down to the beach after a while and bathed, except Mischief, who put one small paw into the water, gave a howl and scampered back up the beach as fast as ever he could, afraid that Tinker might catch him and make him go in! Timmy went in, of course. He swam marvellously, and even gave Tinker a ride on his back, diving down when the boy felt heavy, so that Tinker suddenly found himself sprawling in the water! 'You wretch, Timmy!' yelled the boy. 'The water's gone up my nose. Wait till I catch you! I'll put *you* under!'

But he couldn't possibly catch old Timmy, who really enjoyed the joke. The big dog gave a joyful bark, and swam after George. How he loved being with them all!

The rest of the day went quickly. Jenny had a fine tea for them, with slices of ham, and salad, and fruit to end with, and said afterwards that she had time to play a game of

Scrabble with them if they liked. Mischief sat on the table to watch.

'I don't mind you *watching*,' said Anne. 'But you are NOT to scrabble, Mischief. You sent all my little ivory tiles on the floor last time we played, and I lost the game.'

Timmy watched gravely, sitting on a chair beside George. He simply could NOT understand what made the children play games like this when they could go for a nice long walk with him. They took pity on him when the game was over and went out for a two-mile walk along by the sea. How Timmy loved that!

'I shall cycle to Kirrin Village as soon as it's dark,' announced Julian. 'I suppose your boat is tied up in the usual place, George? I'm sorry I can't take you with me,

149

but there *might* be a bit of danger, as we said. However I won't run into any if I can help it. I shan't feel comfortable until those secret papers are safely out of the way! You can give them to me just before I go, George.'

Anne suddenly yawned. 'Don't start too late or I shall fall asleep!' she said. 'It's getting dark already. All that swimming has made me feel tired!'

Dick yawned too. 'I'm jolly sleepy as well,' he said. 'I shall bed down in our tent as soon as you've gone, Ju. I'll see you off safely first, papers and all! You'd better go to your tent, too, girls – you look tired.'

'Right!' said Anne. 'You coming, George?'

'We'll all go,' said George. 'Come on, Tinker. Bet you I get over the fence and down to our tents first! Good night, Jenny. We're off!'

She and Anne and Tinker, with Timmy running behind, went off down the darkening garden. Dick and Julian helped Jenny to tidy up, and to draw all the curtains. 'Well, good night, Jenny,' said Dick. 'All you have to do is to lock the door behind us and go safely up to bed. We'll go down to our tents now. Sleep well!'

'Oh, I always do,' said Jenny. 'Look after yourselves now and don't get into any mischief! Hide those papers well, where nobody can find them!'

Julian and Dick went off down the garden, having heard Jenny carefully locking the door behind them.

Tinker and the girls were already over the fence, Mischief on Tinker's shoulder. Anne spoke anxiously to

A HAPPY DAY – AND A SHOCK FOR JULIAN

George. 'I do hope Julian will be all right going over to Kirrin Island,' she said. 'I wish he'd take Dick with him.'

'If he took anyone it should be *me*!' burst out George. 'It's *my* island!'

'Oh, don't be silly, George. The papers would be much safer with Julian,' said Anne. 'It would be an awful business for you, cycling by yourself to Kirrin, getting your boat into the water, and rowing over in the dark!'

'It would not!' said George. 'If Julian can do it, then so could I. You go into our tent, Anne, and get ready for bed. I'll come in a minute, after I've taken Timmy for a run.'

She waited till Anne had disappeared through the tent opening. Then she went quietly off by herself in the dark, Timmy trotting beside her, rather surprised.

Soon there came the sound of voices, as Julian and Dick reached the fence and leapt over it. They went to their tent and found Tinker there, yawning and getting ready for bed.

Soon the three boys were all rolled up in their rugs, Mischief cuddled up to Tinker. After some time Julian sat up and looked at his watch, and then peeped out of the tent opening. 'Quite dark!' he said. 'But the moon's coming up, I see. I think I'll get the papers from George now, and set off on my bicycle to Kirrin. I can easily get it out of the shed.'

'You know where George keeps her boat,' said Dick. 'You won't have any difficulty in finding it. Got your torch, Ju?'

'Yes – and a new battery,' said Julian. 'Look!'

He switched on his torch. It gave a good, powerful beam. 'Shan't miss the island if I put *this* on!' he said. 'Now – I'll get those papers. Hey, George – I'm coming to your tent for the papers!'

He went over to the girls' tent. Anne was there, only half-awake. She blinked as Julian's torch shone into her eyes.

'George!' said Julian. 'Give me those papers now, please – hallo – *Hey*, Anne – where is George?'

Anne started looking all round the tent. George's rugs were there, piled in an untidy heap; but there was no George – and no Timmy either!

'Oh, Ju! Do you know what George has done – she's slipped out with the precious papers – and taken Timmy too! She must have gone to fetch her bike, and ridden off to Kirrin to get her boat – and row over to Kirrin Island! Julian, whatever will happen if she rows over and finds somebody waiting to grab those papers from her?' Poor Anne was very near to tears.

'I could *shake* her!' said Julian, very angry indeed. 'Going off alone like that in the dark – cycling to Kirrin – rowing over to the island – and back! She must be mad! Suppose Mr Wooh and his friends are waiting there for her! The – silly – little – idiot!'

'Oh, Julian, quick! You and Dick get your cycles and try to catch her,' begged Anne. 'Oh please do! Anything might happen to her! Dear, silly old George! Thank goodness Timmy's gone with her.'

A HAPPY DAY – AND A SHOCK FOR JULIAN

'Well, that's a blessing, anyway,' said Julian, still angry. 'He'll look after her as much as he can. Oh, I could shake George till her teeth rattled! I *thought* she was rather quiet tonight. Thinking out this plan, I suppose!'

He went up to the house with Dick and Tinker to tell Jenny about George, and then he and Dick at once went to get their bicycles. This was serious. George had no right to be out alone at night like this – and go rowing over to Kirrin Island – ESPECIALLY if there was any chance of someone lying in wait for her!

Jenny was very worried indeed. She watched the two boys cycling off in the dark. Tinker begged her to let him go too, but she wouldn't. 'You and Mischief would just be nuisances,' she said. 'Oh, won't I shake that rascal of a George when she gets back. What a girl! Well, well – thank goodness Timmy's with her. That dog's as good as half a dozen policemen!'

CHAPTER SIXTEEN

Night on Kirrin Island

IT WAS certainly very dark when the half-moon went behind the clouds. George was glad that her bicycle lamp shone so brightly. The shadows in the hedges were deep and mysterious – 'as if they hid people ready to jump out at us,' she said to Timmy. 'But you'd go for them at once, wouldn't you, Timmy!'

Timmy was too much out of breath to bark an answer. George was going pretty fast, and he didn't mean to let her get out of sight. He was sure she shouldn't be out by herself on a dark night like this. He couldn't *imagine* why she had suddenly taken it into her head to go for a long night ride! He raced along, panting.

They met cars with dazzling headlamps, and George had to keep pulling to the side. She was terribly afraid that Timmy might be hit by one of the cars. Oh dear – I'd never, never forgive myself if anything happened to Timmy, she thought. I half wish I hadn't set out now. But I'm NOT going to let Julian hide anything on *my* island. That's my job, not his. 'Timmy darling, PLEASE keep on my left side. You'll be safe then.'

So Timmy kept on her left, still mystified by this sudden journey out into the night. They came at last to Kirrin village, where windows were still lit here and there. Through the village and on to Kirrin Bay – ah, there was the bay! The half-moon slid out from behind a cloud and George saw the dark sea, shining here and there as the moonlight caught the crests of the waves.

'There's my island, look Timmy,' said George, feeling a swelling of pride as she looked over the dark heaving sea to a darker stretch, which she knew was Kirrin Island. 'My very *own* island. Waiting for me tonight!'

'Woof,' said Timmy, rather quietly, because he really hadn't any breath to waste. *Now* what was George going to do? Why had she come out on this lonely ride without the others? Timmy was puzzled.

They came to the stretch of beach where boats were kept. George rode down a ramp to the beach, jumped off her bicycle, and put it by a bathing-hut in the deep shadows. No one would see it there. Then she went to stare over the sea at her island.

She had only looked for a moment or two when she clutched Timmy's collar, and gave an exclamation.

'TIMMY! There's a *light* on my island! Look, to the right there. Can you see it? Timmy, there's somebody camping there. How DARE they? It's *my* island and I don't allow *any*one on it unless they have my permission.'

Timmy looked – and yes, he could see the light too. Was it made by a camp fire – or a lantern? He couldn't tell. All he knew was that he didn't want George to go over there

now. He pawed at her, trying to make her understand that he wanted her to go back home with him.

'No, Timmy. I'm *not* going back till I've found out who's there!' she said. 'It would be cowardly to turn back now. And if it's somebody waiting for me to turn up with the papers, they can think again. Look – I'm hiding them here under the tarpaulin in this boat. It would be idiotic to try and hide them on the island if there's someone there who *might* rob me of anything I've got – it might be one of the thieves who climbed into the tower room, and left some of the papers behind. If *he*'s waiting for me, he won't get any papers!'

George stuffed the parcel of papers under the tarpaulin as she spoke. 'It's Fisherman Connell's boat, called

156

Gypsy,' she said, reading the name on the boat by the light of her torch. '*He* won't mind me hiding something in it!'

She covered up the papers with the tarpaulin, and then looked over to the island again. Yes – that light was still there. Anger welled up in George again, and she went to look for her own boat, which should be somewhere near where they were.

'Here it is,' she said to Timmy, who leapt in at once. She ordered him out for she had to pull the boat down to the water. Fortunately it was a small, light boat and as the tide was almost fully in, she didn't have very far to drag it. Timmy took hold of the rope with his teeth and helped too. At last it was on the water, bobbing gently about in the dim light of the half-moon. Timmy leapt in, and soon George was in too, though with very wet feet!

She took the oars and began to pull away from the shore. 'Tide's almost on the turn,' she told Timmy. 'It won't be too hard a row. Now we can find those campers and tell them what we think of them. You're to bark your very loudest and scare them, Timmy – in fact, you can chase them to their boat, if you like.'

Timmy answered with a small bark. He knew quite well that George didn't want him to make much noise. He thought it was odd that she was going over to her island tonight, all by herself. Why hadn't she taken the others? He was sure that Julian would be very cross!

'Now don't bark or whine, Timmy,' she said, in a whisper. 'We're almost at my landing place – but I'm going under those trees there, not landing here. I want to hide my boat.'

She guided the boat towards some trees whose branches overhung a tiny creek that ran a little way inland. She leapt out, and flung the mooring rope round the trunk of the nearest tree, and made it fast.

'There, little boat,' she said. 'You'll be safe there. No one will see you. Come on, Tim – we'll tackle those campers now.'

She turned to go, and then stopped. 'I wonder where *their* boat is,' she said. 'Let's have a look round, Timmy. It must be here somewhere.'

She soon found the boat lying on the sands, its rope thrown round a nearby rock. The tide was almost up to it. She grinned to herself. 'Timmy!' she whispered. 'I'm going to untie this boat and set it loose on the tide. It will soon be far away. Ha – what will those awful campers say?'

And, to Timmy's amazement, she undid the rope from the rock, rolled it up, and threw the coil inside the boat. Then she gave the boat a push – but it was still embedded in the wet sand.

'Never mind,' she said. 'Another ten minutes and the tide will be right under it – and then it will turn and take the boat with it!'

She began to make her way up the beach, Timmy close to her side. 'Now let's go after those campers, whoever they are,' she said. 'Where's their light gone? I can't see it now.'

But in a minute or two she saw it again. 'It's not from a camp fire – it's from a lantern of some sort,' she whispered to Timmy. 'We'll have to be careful now. Let's see if we can creep up behind them.'

The two of them made their way silently towards the middle of the little island. Here there was an old ruined castle – and there, in the courtyard of the castle, sitting in the midst of thick, overgrown weeds, were two men. George had her hand on Timmy's collar, and tugged it gently. He knew that meant, 'No barking, no growling, Tim,' and he stood perfectly still, the hackles on his neck rising fast.

The two men were playing cards by the light of a fairly powerful lantern, which they had set on a ruined stone wall. Timmy couldn't help giving a surprised growl when he saw one of them, but George hushed him at once.

Mr Wooh, the magician from the circus, was there, dealing out the cards! The other man she didn't know. He was well-dressed, and seemed bored. He flung down his cards as Timmy and George watched from a dark corner of the old castle, and spoke to his companion in an irritated voice.

'Well, whoever it is you said was bringing the rest of those papers here to the island doesn't seem to be turning up. The papers you've given me are good – very good – but of no use without the others. This scientist fellow you've

160

stolen them from is a genius. If we get the complete set of papers, they will be worth a tremendous sum of money, which I can get for you – but without the other papers, there will be no money for you – the first set would be useless!'

'I tell you, someone will be here with them. I heard them say so,' said Mr Wooh in his stately voice.

'Who stole them – you?' asked the other man, shuffling the cards quickly.

'No. I did not steal them,' said Mr Wooh. 'Me, I keep my hands clean – I do not steal.'

The second man laughed. 'No. You let other people do your dirty work for you, don't you! Mr Wooh, the World's Most Wonderful Magician, does not soil his hands! He merely uses the hands of others – and charges enormous prices for the goods they steal. You're a cunning one, Mr Wooh. I wouldn't like you for an enemy! How did you manage to get the papers?'

'By using my eyes and my ears and my cunning,' answered Mr Wooh. 'They are better than most people's. So many people are stupid, my good friend.'

'I'm not your good friend,' said the other man. 'I've *got* to do business with you, Mr Wooh, but I wouldn't like to have you for a friend. I'd rather have that chimpanzee of yours! I don't even like playing cards with you! *WHY* doesn't this fellow come?'

George put her mouth to one of Timmy's ears. 'Timmy, I'm going to tell them to clear off my island,' she whispered furiously to the listening dog. 'Fancy fellows like *that* daring to set foot here – rascals and rogues! Don't come with me – wait till I call you, then if you have to rescue me, come at once!'

Leaving a most unwilling Timmy standing beside part of the old castle wall, she suddenly appeared before the two astonished men by the light of their lantern.

They leapt to their feet at once. 'It's the girl who's come – I shouldn't have thought that the boys would have let her,' said Mr Wooh, astonished. 'I am . . .'

'WHAT ARE YOU DOING ON MY ISLAND?' demanded George, angrily. 'It belongs to *me*. I saw your light and came over with my dog. Be careful of him – he's big and strong and fierce. Clear off at once, or I'll report you to the police!'

'Easy, easy, now!' said Mr Wooh, standing very straight and looking immensely tall. 'So the boys sent *you* to hide the papers instead of daring to come themselves. How cowardly of them! Where are the papers? Give them to me.'

'I've hidden them,' said George. 'They're not very far away. You didn't think I'd be silly enough to come along to you with them in my hands when I saw your light and knew that people were here, did you? No – I've hidden them somewhere on the shore – where *you* won't find them. Now you just clear off, both of you!'

'A very brave and determined young lady!' said Mr Wooh, bowing solemnly to George.

'Do you mean to tell me that's a *girl*!' said the other man, amazed. 'Well! She's a plucky kid, I must say! Look here, kid, if you've got those papers, hand them over, and I'll give you a whole lot of money which you can give to Professor Hayling with my best wishes.'

'Come and get them,' said George, turning as if to go. The two men looked at one another, eyebrows raised. Mr Wooh nodded, and then winked. If George had seen his face she would have known what that wink meant. It meant let's humour this silly kid, follow her – see the hiding place, snatch the papers and clear off in our boat without paying a penny! But LOOK OUT for the dog!

George led the way, Timmy walking between her and the two men. He was growling all the time, deep down in his throat, as if to say 'Just you lay a finger on George and

FIVE ARE TOGETHER AGAIN

I'll bite it off!' The men took care not to go too near him! They shone the lantern on him all the time, making sure that he was not going to leap at them.

George led them to the shore, to the place where they had left their boat. Mr Wooh gave a cry. 'Where's our boat? It was tied to that rock!'

'Is this it over this ridge?' called George climbing up a steep bank that overhung the water, which was now quite deep with the surging tide.

The men went to look – and then George gave them the surprise of their lives! She ran at Mr Wooh and gave him such a push that he fell right over the high bank into the sea below, landing with a yell and a terrific splash. George shouted a command to Timmy, who was now very excited, and the big dog did the same to the other man, leaping at him and pushing him over. He, too, shot over the ridge and fell into the sea with a splash. Timmy stood on the little cliff and barked madly, as excited as George.

'You'll have to swim to the shore of the mainland if you want to escape!' yelled George. 'The tide has taken away your boat – I set it loose! You'd better not get back on my island yet – Timmy's on the watch for you – and he'll fly at either of you if you try to set a foot on it again!'

Both men could swim, though not very well, and both were exceedingly angry and very frightened. They were sure they could never swim to the mainland – but how to get on the island to safety, they didn't know. That great, fierce dog was there, barking as if he wanted to bite them

into small bits. Their boat had been set loose, there was no way to escape. They swam round in circles, not knowing what to do!

'I'm going back to the mainland now!' yelled George, climbing into her boat. 'I'll send the police to rescue you in the morning. You can get on my island now – but you're in for a VERY cold night! Goodbye!'

And off went George in her boat, with Timmy standing at the back, watching to make sure those men didn't swim after them. He gave George an admiring lick. She wasn't afraid of ANYTHING! He'd rather belong to *her* than to anyone else in the world. WOOF, WOOF, W-O-O-F!

CHAPTER SEVENTEEN

And at last the mystery is solved!

GEORGE COULDN'T help singing loudly as she rowed back to the shore in her boat. Timmy joined in with a bark now and again. He was glad that George was so happy. He stood in the prow of the boat, wishing it was not night time, so that he could see clearly where he was going. The moon clouded over, and the sea looked endless in the dark. Very few lights showed on the mainland at that time of night – just one or two from houses where people were still up.

Wait, though – what was that bright light suddenly shining out from the mainland? Was it someone trying to pick out their boat? Timmy barked at the light, and George, who, of course, was rowing with her back to the shore, shipped her oars for a moment and looked round.

'It's someone on the quay,' she said. 'Maybe a late fisherman. Good! He'll be able to help me drag my boat up out of the way of the tide!'

But it wasn't a fisherman. It was Julian and Dick. They had arrived about five minutes ago, and had looked at once for George's boat and hadn't found it. 'Bother! We're too late to stop her, then. She's gone over to the island!'

said Julian and began to examine all the other tied-up boats to see if he could find one that he could borrow, belonging to a friend. *Somehow* they must get over to Kirrin Island, and rescue George. He felt sure she would be in danger of some kind.

Then suddenly the two boys heard the sounds of oars splashing not far out to sea. Well, if that was a fisherman coming home, maybe Julian could ask *him* to lend him his boat to go to Kirrin Island in. He could tell him that he was afraid his cousin might be in need of help.

Timmy, in George's boat, suddenly recognised the two boys when the moon swam out from a cloud, and gave a delighted volley of barks. George, wondering if it *was* Julian and Dick, rowed as quickly as she could. She came into shore, jumped out and began to drag in her boat. The boys were beside her at once, and the boat was soon in its usual place, carefully made safe in case the tide was a high one.

'George!' said Julian, so overjoyed to see his cousin safe and sound that he couldn't help giving her a bear hug. 'You wicked girl! You went to the island – just what I said you *weren't* to do. You might have found the thieves on the island, and *then* you would have been in trouble!'

'I *did* find them – but it's *they* who are in trouble, not me!' said George. 'I saw a light over there, took my boat and went over to the island – and there they were – Mr Wooh the Magician and another man – ON MY IS-LAND! Did you ever hear such cheek? They asked me for the papers at once!'

AND AT LAST THE MYSTERY IS SOLVED!

'Oh, George – did you give them to the men?' asked Dick.

'Of *course* not! I'd already hidden them where those men couldn't possibly find them. I wasn't idiotic enough to take them over to hide on the *island* when I saw somebody was there – probably waiting for me – *and* for the papers!' said George.

'But, George – if you knew somebody was there, why on *earth* did you risk going over to Kirrin Island then?' asked Julian, puzzled. 'It was a very dangerous thing to do.'

'I wanted to turn off whoever it was, of course,' said George. 'As if I'd allow just *anyone* on my island! It's mine, my very own, and I only allow people on it that I like. You know that.'

'I just NEVER know what you'll do next, George,' said Julian, patting Timmy on the head. 'How did you *dare* to go and tackle those men? Oh, I know Timmy was with you, but even so . . . why in the world didn't the men row after you, and ram your boat?'

'Well, you see, they couldn't,' said George. 'I found their boat, untied it, and set it adrift on the tide. It's probably half a mile away by now!'

The boys were so astonished that they couldn't even laugh at first. But then, when they thought of the two men marooned on Kirrin Island, their boat gone goodness knows where, they laughed till tears came into their eyes!

'George, I don't know how you can *think* of doing such things!' said Julian. 'Weren't the men furious?'

'I don't know,' said George. 'I didn't tell them about their boat. I pretended that I'd take them to where I'd hidden the papers – and then when we got on to a nice high ridge overlooking the sea, they looked over it to see if their boat was all right, and I gave Mr Wooh a jolly good push, and Timmy leapt at the man with him – and in they went – SPLASH! SPLASH!'

Julian really *had* to sit down and have another bout of laughing till the stitch in his side grew so bad that he was forced to get up and walk about. George suddenly saw the funny side of it all too, and she began to laugh as heartily as Julian. Dick joined in as well, and Timmy barked madly, enjoying the fun.

'Oh dear!' said Julian, feeling weak with laughter, 'and then I suppose you said a polite farewell and left them to their fate?'

'Well, actually I yelled out to tell them I'd send the police to rescue them in the morning,' said George. 'I'm afraid they'll both spend a very uncomfortable night – they were soaking wet, you see!'

'George – I'm beginning to think it was a good thing *you* went with the papers to the island, and not me, after all,' said Julian. 'I should *never* have thought of doing all the things you did – pushing the men into the sea – really, how *could* you and Timmy dare to do such things? And setting their boat loose! What on earth will the police say when we tell them?'

'I don't think we'd better tell them, had we?' said

AND AT LAST THE MYSTERY IS SOLVED!

George. 'I mean – they might think I'd gone too far. Anyway, why not let the two men kick their heels on the island all night, and we'll decide what to do about the police in the morning. It's funny – I suddenly feel awfully tired.'

'I bet you do!' said Dick. 'Come on, let's get our bikes. Oh, and those precious papers – where are they?'

'Under the tarpaulin in Fisherman Connell's boat,' said George, and suddenly gave the most enormous yawn. 'I hid them there.'

'I'll get them,' said Julian. 'Then off we go back to Big Hollow House. The others will be getting awfully worried by now!'

He found the papers in the fishing boat and then the three of them rode off quickly along the road from Kirrin to Big Hollow, Timmy running behind them. Julian kept laughing to himself. George was amazing! Fancy tackling those two fellows like that – pushing them into the water, and setting their boat adrift. Julian was sure he would never have thought of doing such daring things himself.

At last they were back at the tents, and the others crowded round them to hear what had happened. Anne looked very white. Jenny was with her, comforting her – she had *just* made up her mind to telephone the police, and was *most* relieved to see George again.

'We'll tell you all the details in the morning,' said Julian. 'But all I'll say now is that the papers are safe all right, here in my pocket – the thieves were probably Mr Wooh and another man. They were on the island tonight, waiting for George. They *had* overheard what she said in the tent! However, George and Timmy pushed them both into the water and set their boat adrift, so things are settling down nicely! They will have to spend the night on the island, cold and wet through!'

'*George* did all that!' said Jenny, amazed. 'Well! I never knew she was so *dangerous*! Good gracious! I feel right-down scared of her! Settle down to sleep in your tent, dear – you look tired out!'

George was glad to flop down on her rugs. Now that the excitement was all over she felt too sleepy for words! She fell asleep at once – but Julian and Dick didn't. They lay awake for some time, chuckling over George's deeds of daring. What a cousin to have!

When they were up at the house at breakfast next morning, Jeremy came up the garden and put his head in at the dining-room window. 'Hey!' he said. 'Mr Wooh's not in his tent this morning! He's disappeared! And poor old Charlie the Chimp is too miserable for words.'

'Ah – we can tell you *exactly* where Mr Wooh is,' said Julian. 'But – wait a bit, Tinker, where are you going? You haven't finished your . . .'

But Tinker had gone off with Jeremy at top speed! He was very fond of Charlie. Oh dear, would the chimpanzee weep for his master and refuse to take his food? Tinker called Mischief and they both ran down to the fence with Jeremy and climbed over it. Tinker went straight to

AND AT LAST THE MYSTERY IS SOLVED!

Charlie's cage. The chimpanzee sat with his head in his hands, rocking himself to and fro, making sad, crying noises.

'Let's get into the cage with him,' said Tinker. 'He'll like to be comforted. He must be missing Mr Wooh very, very much.'

They crawled into the cage and sat down in the straw, each putting an arm round the sad chimpanzee. Old Grandad was very surprised to see them both there.

'Don't know what's happened to Mr Wooh,' he said. 'Didn't come home last night! Here, Jeremy, you come on out. I can't spare you to cry over Charlie all morning. He'll soon perk up. *You* can stay with him, Tinker, if you like.'

Jeremy crawled out of the cage and went off crossly. Tinker sat with his arm round Charlie, wishing he didn't look so terribly sad. As he sat there, he heard a funny little noise going on all the time. Tick-tick-tick-ticka-ticka-tick-tick-tick-tick-ticka-ticka-tick. 'Sounds like a watch or something,' said Tinker, and scrabbled about in the straw. Perhaps Mr Wooh's big gold watch had fallen into Charlie's cage?

His hand felt something small and round and smooth at the bottom of the cage. He riffled away the thick straw, and drew out the object underneath it. He stared and stared at it in the utmost surprise. Charlie saw him looking at it, snatched it away and hid it in the straw again. He made a few growly noises as if he were angry.

AND AT LAST THE MYSTERY IS SOLVED!

'Charlie, *where* did you get that little clock?' said Tinker. 'Oh, CHARLIE! Well, as you're so sad this morning, I'll give it to you for your very own. Just to cheer you up. But oh, Charlie, I *am* surprised at you!'

He slid out of the cage and went back over the fence and into his own garden. Up the path he ran and burst into the dining-room, where the others were still finishing their breakfast.

'What's up?' said Dick.

'Listen! I know who the thief was who climbed in at the tower window . . . I KNOW WHO HE WAS!' cried Tinker, almost shouting in his excitement.

'WHO?' said everyone, in amazement.

'It was CHARLIE THE CHIMP!' said Tinker. 'Why didn't we think of him before? He can climb anything! It would be quite easy for *him* to swing himself up that rough-stoned wall, hanging on to the bits of creeper here and there – and to the uneven stones – and climb through the window into the tower room, collect all the papers he could hold – and climb down again – *slither* down again, probably . . .'

'THAT must have been the slithering sound I heard!' said Jenny. 'I *told* you I heard a queer slithering noise!'

'And the whispering you heard must have been Mr Wooh trying to make him go up the tower wall and into the window!' said Julian. 'Gosh – I bet poor old Charlie's been taught to get into all sorts of windows and take whatever he sees. Mr Wooh must have known

Tinker's father worked out all his ideas up in the tower.'

'Wooh could easily teach him to take papers,' said Julian. 'But there were, of course, too many for old Charlie in the tower room. He wouldn't be able to carry them *all* in his front paws, for he needed *all* his paws to climb down that steep wall – so he must have crammed as many as he could into his mouth – and dropped the rest under the table! Charlie the Chimp – well! Who would have thought *he* could be the thief!'

'Wait a bit – how on earth do you know it was Charlie?' said Dick. 'Nobody saw him. It was at night.'

'Well, I *do* know it was Charlie,' said Tinker. 'You remember that dear little clock on the tower room mantelpiece? Well, it disappeared on the night when those papers were stolen – and *I* found it hidden in the straw in Charlie's cage this morning! He snatched it away from me, and almost cried – so I let him keep it! It was ticking loudly just like it always did. It was the loud ticking that told me it was there in the cage!'

'Who wound it up at nights, to keep it going?' said Julian, at once, most astonished.

'Charlie, I suppose,' said Tinker. 'He's very clever with his paws! The clock was quite safe, hidden in his cage. Nobody would be likely to get into the chimp's cage and sit there with him – but *I* did this morning, and that's how I found it. I heard it ticking, you see. I bet old Charlie was clever enough to pop his precious clock into his mouth when he saw any of the men coming to clean out his cage!'

'Well, I'm blessed!' said Jenny. 'How was it that Mr Wooh never saw him bringing it along with the papers that night, when he stole them?'

'Well, as Tinker told you – my guess is that old Charlie must have put the little clock in his mouth then, along with the papers,' said Dick. 'He needed all his four paws, climbing – or rather *slithering* down that wall – and he's got a jolly big mouth! You should see what a lot of food he can stuff into it!'

'Yes. And Mr Wooh would take the papers, of course – Charlie would just take them from his mouth and hand them to him – but he'd be crafty enough to keep his precious new toy hidden in his mouth! Poor old Charlie! Can't you see him listening to the clock, and cuddling it – like a child with a new toy!' said George.

'He sounded exactly as if he were crying this morning,' said Tinker. 'I couldn't bear it. Poor old Charlie! He couldn't understand *why* Mr Wooh didn't go and see him today. He was *so* miserable!'

'I think we'll *have* to get the police along now,' said Julian. 'Not only to catch Mr Wooh and his friend, left so conveniently marooned by George on her island – but also because Mr Wooh should be charged with stealing your father's irreplaceable charts and diagrams, Tinker. Goodness knows what else he has taught poor old Charlie to steal. I bet he's sent the chimp into a lot of houses, and up many walls, and into many windows.'

'Yes. There's probably been a trail of robberies wherever the circus went,' said Jenny. 'And many innocent people must have been suspected.'

'What a shame!' said Anne. 'But, oh dear – if Mr Wooh goes to prison, whatever will become of poor old Charlie the Chimp?'

'I bet Jeremy will take him,' said Tinker. 'He loves him, and old Charlie adores Jeremy! He'll be all right with Jeremy and old Grandad!'

'Well, Tinker, I think you'd better go and tell your father all this,' said Jenny. 'I know he's busy – he always is – but this is a thing *he* ought to deal with and nobody else. If you'd like to fetch him, George could tell him the whole story – and then I rather guess *he'll* ring up the police – and Mr Wooh will find himself in a whole lot of trouble.'

So there goes Tinker, with Mischief on his shoulder, to find his father, down the hall – up the stairs – along the landing – into his father's bedroom . . . R-r-r-r-r-r-r-r-r-r-r-r! Tinker, you sound like a motor-scooter going up a steep hill! PARP-PARP! *Don't* hoot like that, you'll make your father so angry that he won't listen to a word you say!

But the Professor *did* listen – and soon Jenny heard him telephoning the police. They're coming straight away, and that means that Mr Wooh the Magician is in for a most unpleasant time, and his magic won't help him at all! He'll have to give back the papers that he made Charlie steal –

AND AT LAST THE MYSTERY IS SOLVED!

and plenty of other things, too! There he is, marooned on the island, quite unable to escape, waiting fearfully with his companion, for the police!

'Another adventure over!' said George, with a regretful sigh. 'And a jolly exciting one too! I'm glad you solved the mystery, Tinker – it was clever of you to find the little tower room clock. I bet Mr Wooh wouldn't have let Charlie keep it, if he'd known he'd taken it from the tower room! Poor old Charlie the Chimp!'

'I'm just wondering if Dad would let me keep Charlie here, while Mr Wooh is in prison,' began Tinker, and stopped as Jenny gave a horrified shriek.

'*Tinker*! If you so much as *mention* that idea to your father, I'll walk straight out of this house and NEVER COME BACK!' said Jenny. 'That chimp would be in my kitchen all day long – oh yes, he would – and things would be disappearing out of my larder, and my cupboards, and my drawers, and he'd dance up and down and scream at me if I so much as said a word, and . . .'

'All right, dear, dear Jenny, I won't ask for Charlie, honest I won't,' said Tinker. 'I do love you a *bit* more than I'd love a chimp – but think what a companion he would be for Mischief!'

'I'm not thinking anything of the sort!' said Jenny. 'And what about you taking a bit of notice of that monkey of yours – bless us all if he hasn't helped himself to half that jar of jam – just *look* at his sticky face! Oh, what a week this has been, what with chimps

179

and monkeys and children and robberies, and George disappearing, and all!'

'Dear old Jenny,' said George, laughing as she went off into the kitchen. 'What an exciting time we've had! I really did enjoy every minute of it!'

So did we, George. Hurry up and fall into another adventure. We are longing to hear what you and the others will be up to next. How we wish we could join you! Goodbye for now – and take care of yourselves, Five. Good luck!

A complete list of the FAMOUS FIVE ADVENTURES *by Enid Blyton*

1 FIVE ON A TREASURE ISLAND
2 FIVE GO ADVENTURING AGAIN
3 FIVE RUN AWAY TOGETHER
4 FIVE GO TO SMUGGLER'S TOP
5 FIVE GO OFF IN A CARAVAN
6 FIVE ON KIRRIN ISLAND AGAIN
7 FIVE GO OFF TO CAMP
8 FIVE GET INTO TROUBLE
9 FIVE FALL INTO ADVENTURE
10 FIVE ON A HIKE TOGETHER
11 FIVE HAVE A WONDERFUL TIME
12 FIVE GO DOWN TO THE SEA
13 FIVE GO TO MYSTERY MOOR
14 FIVE HAVE PLENTY OF FUN
15 FIVE ON A SECRET TRAIL
16 FIVE GO TO BILLYCOCK HILL
17 FIVE GET INTO A FIX
18 FIVE ON FINNISTON FARM
19 FIVE GO TO DEMON'S ROCKS
20 FIVE HAVE A MYSTERY TO SOLVE
21 FIVE ARE TOGETHER AGAIN

If you enjoyed this Famous Five centenary edition, you'll enjoy:

FIVE GO ADVENTURING AGAIN
Enid Blyton

A thief at Kirrin Cottage! Who can it be? The Famous Five think they know – but they need proof! Then they find an old map and an unusual hiding place . . .

If you enjoyed this Famous Five centenary edition, you'll enjoy:

FIVE RUN AWAY TOGETHER
Enid Blyton

Who's been on George's island? And what is locked in the mysterious trunk hidden on Kirrin Island? The Famous Five think they're on the trail of smugglers – until they hear a child scream . . .

If you enjoyed this Famous Five centenary edition, you'll enjoy:

FIVE GO TO SMUGGLER'S TOP
Enid Blyton

Are there still smugglers at Smuggler's Top? The Famous Five go to stay at the large, old house and discover hiding places and underground tunnels! Then they catch people signalling out to sea – who can they be?